Ava watched Luca
step onto the slick surface of the ice.

He teetered slightly before finding his balance. Face fixed in concentration, he moved slowly toward her.

"Hold on, Ava. I'll be there in a minute."

She watched through blurry eyes as he stepped onto the chunk of ice near her. She was amazed that he had not fallen through. Her body shivered so bad she could hardly keep him in her field of vision.

"Please go back," she whispered.

Slowly, kneeling on a shelf of ice, he crouched over to grab for her sleeve. The green of his eyes was the only thing she could see clearly. His fingers gripped her wrist and he hauled her toward him, hoisting her over his shoulder. Ava wanted to say something, to force her body to work in some way, but she could not. She found herself slung head down, staring at the milky ice beneath Luca's feet.

And then, with a sudden lurch, they both plunged through the ice.

Books by Dana Mentink

Love Inspired Suspense

Killer Cargo
Flashover
Race to Rescue
Endless Night
Betrayal in the Badlands
Turbulence
Buried Truth
Escape from the Badlands
*Lost Legacy
*Dangerous Melody
*Final Resort

*Treasure Seekers

DANA MENTINK

lives in California, where the weather is golden and the cheese is divine. Her family includes two girls (affectionately nicknamed Yogi and Boo Boo). Papa Bear works for the fire department; he met Dana doing a dinner theater production of *The Velveteen Rabbit.* Ironically, their parts were husband and wife.

Dana is a 2009 American Christian Fiction Writers Book of the Year finalist for romantic suspense and an award winner in the Pacific Northwest Writers Literary Contest. Her novel *Betrayal in the Badlands* won a 2010 *RT Book Reviews* Reviewers' Choice Award. She has enjoyed writing a mystery series for Barbour Books and more than ten novels to date for Harlequin's Love Inspired Suspense line.

She spent her college years competing in speech and debate tournaments all around the country. Besides writing, she busies herself teaching elementary school and reviewing books for her blog. Mostly, she loves to be home with her family, including a dog with social-anxiety problems, a chubby box turtle and a quirky parakeet.

Dana loves to hear from her readers via her website at www.danamentink.com.

FINAL RESORT

DANA MENTINK

Love Inspired

Recycling programs
for this product may
not exist in your area.

™ LOVE INSPIRED BOOKS

ISBN-13: 978-0-373-67547-0

FINAL RESORT

www.LoveInspiredBooks.com

Printed in U.S.A.

Again, the kingdom of heaven
is like a merchant seeking fine pearls,
and upon finding one pearl of great value,
he went and sold all that he had, and bought it.
—*Matthew* 13:45–46

To my Mike, who is a priceless treasure to me.

ONE

"Again, the kingdom of heaven is like a merchant seeking fine pearls, and when he had found one of great value, he went and sold all that he had, and bought it."

—*Matthew 13: 45-46*

Ava Stanton jumped when a bevy of quail scattered as she got out of the car, snow whisking in tiny puffs under their feet. One shot her a beady-eyed look as if to ask why in the world a woman would be out on the remote mountain road by herself, especially as another wave of winter storms rolled in across the Sierras. Ava wondered the same thing, pulling her knit cap farther down over her short blond hair. The family of quail left a profound silence behind as they moved away. In the distance, she caught the sound of skiers on the slopes of the neighboring Gold Summit Lodge which butted up against Whisper Mountain Resort property.

Won't be our property much longer.

The thought sent a wave of despair through her. She shook it off. Too much coffee. Too little sleep. She was fatigued mentally and physically from the extra skiing classes she'd been teaching in West-bow, a town about twenty miles away where she rented a room. A useless effort. Hadn't made a dent in the debt that buried Whisper Mountain.

The sky was cloudy and ominous. Shadows shifted on the lumps of snow that had collected on the steep slope overlooking an iced-over Melody Lake at the periphery of the Whisper Mountain Resort property.

She did not know the real name of the lake, only the nickname given to the small body of water by her uncle the day they'd scattered her mother's ashes there, accompanied by the mournful singing of the birds. Melody Lake. How often she'd visited, watching the seasons morph from summer to the white cocoon of winter, the water gradually sealing over like her own grief. Sealed over, but still just as present.

The delicate cover of ice sparkled at her.

Thin ice.

How appropriate. Whatever her uncle Paul was involved in this time, he was no doubt teetering on the edge of another disaster. There was hardly much left to lose. Whisper Mountain was officially defunct, closed at the cusp of the ski season because there was no longer money enough to maintain the slopes and lodge. They'd kept the toboggan run open the past several years, but now there was not even money to keep that going. Thanks in part to Uncle Paul's penchant for disastrous get-rich-quick schemes, the land would have to be sold without further delay. Looking along the graceful peaks adorned with white-crusted fir trees, her heart squeezed painfully. It was still Stanton-owned, at least for a few more months.

Again she looked toward the distant slopes of Gold Summit, partially owned by the wealthy Gage family. The rumor mill held that Luca, one of the sons, and his sister were visiting. Luca's green eyes and infectious grin twirled in her memory. She'd read that he'd started a treasure hunting business. The perfect job for a guy perpetually in motion. When times were better, her father had frequently hosted marshmallow roasts attended by Wyatt Gage and his then-teen children. Happy days. Long gone.

She got back into the car to check her phone. She reread Paul's old text, replete with errors.

Found my purl. Meet me at yer mothers lake. Secret.

What was it this time? Uncle Paul referred to his "pearl" for as long as she'd known him, a term applied to every treasure in the long list he'd pursued over the years. A new stock market tip? An undiscovered platinum mine that would save their bankrupt Whisper Mountain Resort? His latest woman? During his last phone call, he refused to talk other than to say he'd contact her soon. Not like the jovial Uncle Paul, the trickster, the showman.

She caught the sound of a set of boots crunching down the road. Uncle Paul appeared, wild black hair threaded with silver curling from under his red knit cap. He saw her and waved, looking around carefully before he marched down the slope to meet her.

He clasped her in a bear hug, cold cheek pressed to hers. "Avy, honey. You get more gorgeous every time I see you." He pulled away to look into her face. "It's those blue eyes. Like perfect lapis lazuli. Remind me of a set of stones I picked up in Myanmar."

She could not resist the flattery and bestowed a kiss on his cheek. "All right. It's only been a couple of months since we were together, so you don't need to go overboard. I didn't even know you were back in California." She looked for her uncle's ever-present shadow. "Where's Mack Dog?"

"In the truck."

Uncle Paul pointed to the top of the hill. She could just make out a glimmer of his dented pickup.

"He's getting old now. Doesn't like snow in his paws." He sighed. "Me, too, getting old. Been thinking about a lot of things lately."

The edge of melancholy in his words was so unlike him. "Where have you been? Why did you want to meet me?" She shivered and pulled her scarf tighter. "If you're going to try to talk me out of selling the place, it won't work. I've been the legal owner since I turned twenty-five two years ago."

"Yes, I am, but not for the reason you think." His eyes flickered over the frozen lake below them. He sighed, long and low, a sound so mournful that Ava felt a sudden twinge of dread.

"We don't have any choice but to sell it," she began, readying for yet another argument. "Dad thinks so, too." Her father had thought so for years and hadn't been shy about his opinions. She wished he was here now, but the winters were too harsh for a paraplegic in his condition.

He cut her off with a wave of his mittened hand.

"Ava, I know I messed up. Your mother left this place to us, and I took advantage. I blew it. Took money out figuring I could make it back and then some, but I never did."

She hated the tone of defeat in her uncle's voice. "You meant no harm. I know that."

He shook his head, sending a sprinkling of snow loose into the air that mingled with the flakes just starting to fall. "In my mind I knew I could make Whisper sparkle by the time you were old enough to take the reins, to bring it back to the days when there were people all over the mountain and wagon rides and campfires at midnight. You remember?"

"I remember."

"I know I was a wedge between your father and

mother. Maybe if I'd stayed away, been more responsible, things would have turned out differently."

"My father would still be disabled from the wreck, and Mom would still have given up." She heard the bitter edge in her own words.

Uncle Paul heard it, too. The lines around his mouth deepened.

He flicked a glance toward the ridge above them where clouds massed in fantastic formation. "This time I really found it." He moved closer and took her by the shoulders. "As soon as I get it authenticated, we're going to have enough money to save Whisper Mountain with plenty left over."

Ava knew enough not to feed into her uncle's pie-in-the-sky notions. Even though she was barely twenty-seven, she had to be the mature voice of reason. "Whatever you think you've found, leave it where it is. I'm selling. I've got no choice."

He looked behind them at the stretch of road that meandered up to the top of the next hill separating Whisper Mountain from Gold Summit, immediately to the west of them. A lacy curtain of snow had begun to fall, the flakes blown around them by a frigid wind.

"Why did we have to meet here?" she demanded again.

He shrugged, but she thought she saw a shimmer of fear in his eyes. "Proper thing, to tell you here that Whisper Mountain is saved. I come here to pray all the time and you used to, didn't you, Ave? Do you still come?"

She shook her head. "Not anymore." Whisper Mountain was a place dead to her, buried in the past. The only reason she'd returned from Westbow was to sell it. Snow settled onto her lashes and she brushed it away.

She'd lost too much because of her mother's suicide ten years before. Ava's own life would forever be bisected by her mother's decision, into the time when she had been a normal, happy teen and after, when the world became an uncertain place. The source of her pain was right here on this piece of snow-covered world, and she was finally going to let it go.

"Uncle Paul, tell me—" she broke off as he started visibly, body tense.

"Did you hear that?"

"What?" she said, trying to pinpoint the source of his concern.

"I thought I heard Mack Dog. He must have gotten out and gone wandering again."

They both stood motionless, listening. The sound of an engine floated through the air and a snowmobile appeared at the bottom of the slope.

Paul's eyes narrowed in suspicion.

"Who is that?" she asked.

The snowmobile took off in their direction, gaining speed as it went. Ava stood frozen as it barreled toward them. Surely, the driver would stop, slow down as he approached.

He didn't. Incredibly, he seemed only to increase his speed. Paul shoved Ava away. "Get in the car."

"Wait," she screamed as Paul took off heading for the trees.

The snowmobile roared closer, changing course to target Uncle Paul.

"Get away, Ava," Uncle Paul yelled over his shoulder. "Get away now."

Luca looked over the pristine slope, skis poised to begin the descent. He could not keep from turning his gaze to the valley down below, ringed with hills. He remembered his high school winter breaks spent skiing here. His heart replayed the memory of the young woman who was so at home on the snow she seemed to fly over it, like a hawk skimming over the crystal world below. He was proficient on skis but never as good as she was, not even close. He wondered if she ever visited here, now that her property was closed up. Everything had changed her senior year after the car accident crippled her father and her mother committed suicide six months later.

"Hey, there," Stephanie said softly. "Lost in thought?"

He avoided looking at his sister. Even though he was elated that she and her high school sweetheart, Tate, had reunited in the course of their last treasure hunt, the happiness that shone on her face reminded him that he had just ended things with a woman he'd dated casually. There was no spark there, no spring of devotion like he'd seen in the eyes of his sister when she talked about Tate. "No, just remembering how good the runs were on Whisper Mountain."

She didn't answer, pushing a strand of her short dark hair back under her ski cap, gazing into the distance at the empty slopes. "It's a prime piece of real estate. Do you think Dad will buy it?"

He nodded. "I think he'd be a fool not to. Anyway, let's get some slope time before Victor lines up our new mission." Victor was the eldest Gage sibling and recently married in a double wedding along with Tate and Stephanie. It was fitting, as their last job at Treasure Seekers had turned up an eighteen-million-dollar violin and nearly gotten them all killed at the hands of a psychopath. They were all due for some good times.

Stephanie shivered, and he knew she was reliving the memories of their near escape, too. "Let's get back. Tate's probably missing us."

Luca grinned. "Missing you. We're still not best buds."

"That's because you're both stubborn gorillas."

"True, but he's your stubborn gorilla now, and he looks at you like he can't believe you're really his."

She blushed. "It drives him crazy that his bum leg keeps him down there while I'm up here, so I suspect he's strong-armed someone into giving him a pair of skis. I'd better get back before he thinks he's ready for the expert slopes."

"You go on," Luca said with a chuckle. "I'm going to take it slow. Meet you down there."

"Take it slow? Since when?" Stephanie cocked her head and gave him that look. "Sure?"

"Sure."

"All right, but don't do anything crazy on the slopes. There's a storm coming in. Remember, you're a treasure hunter, not an Olympic athlete." She swished away down the hill, skis gliding smoothly over the sparkling ground.

She was right, he was a treasure hunter at heart and it had been his idea to form the Treasure Seekers agency in the first place. He'd told himself it was to help his brother Victor deal with his first wife's sudden death, but it was more than likely a way to soothe his constant restlessness. In the off season when he wasn't piloting a helicopter for the U.S. Forest Service, there was not enough to keep him busy and busy was the only thing that kept him sane. He was the kid in grade school who could never seem to stay in his seat. Some things hadn't changed.

He and his siblings had found treasures, all right, everything from lost masterpieces to priceless stamps, yet he always experienced a letdown after each case, as if the treasure, rich though it was, was somehow not the prize he was meant to be looking for.

"Earthly treasures aren't going to satisfy," he could hear his father say. But he felt so alive when he was deep in the throes of a search, however dissatisfying the ending might be.

He shook the thoughts away and pulled his goggles into place.

One more run.

He shouldn't be skiing here, so close to the shutdown Whisper property. He puzzled over why the fond memories of his past there felt so strong. Idly he wondered what Ava would do after her family's property was sold. At least the sale might afford them some security. That's what Luca's father believed when he proposed buying it pending Luca's report.

Head out of the clouds, Luca.

He mentally picked out the path he intended to take down the mountain and readied himself to push off.

A streak of black caught his attention.

He jerked toward the movement, thinking he had imagined it until the shape zinged again through the white-robed trees finally coming to a stop on a flat rock that protruded above the snow. The dog barked, a loud, agitated sound that cut through the quiet of the snow-covered hollow.

Luca stared at the animal. Even though he could not figure out what a dog would be doing alone out here on the slopes, he was far more surprised by one particular detail. The animal was big, a scruffy black-and-tan creature that spoke of German shepherd parentage with something fluffier mixed in, but the strangest thing about him was his left ear, the top of which had been cut off somehow long ago, leaving a flattened tip.

Luca had known a dog with just such an ear, but he could not believe it. Ava's dreamer of an uncle owned a critter that answered to the same description, but it could not be one and the same. Uncle Paul, last Luca had heard, was lying low to escape a group of unsavory folks from whom he'd borrowed money.

"Mack Dog?" Luca yelled out, amazed that he remembered the name.

The dog jerked as if he'd gotten a shock, stood up and wagged a tentative tail in Luca's direction.

A noise from over the hill made them both tense. Luca was not sure but it might have been a shout or maybe just the echo of some agitated bird.

Mack Dog leaped from the rock, floundering in the snow before he began an awkward journey in the direction of the noise, bulldozing his way through the frozen piles, standing every few feet on his rear legs to get his visual bearings.

Luca watched the dog in amazement.

How could it be Mack Dog?

He listened again, heard a snowmobile engine. Just someone enjoying the slopes like himself, who had probably lost track of his dog. He should ski on, go to meet his sister, but something turned him in a different direction, toward a smooth section that would take him to the source of the noise.

Mack Dog, or whoever's dog it might be, wouldn't survive long left alone on the mountain. Luca poled out to a promising spot and skied as quickly as he could manage downslope, where he edged into a turn that would take him toward the hill. He could make out Mack Dog barreling through the trees in the same direction.

The slope was not as smooth as he made the turn, the snow uneven and bumpy. He had to use his poles vigorously to keep the momentum, and his breath came in white puffs. Finally he made it to a spot where he could see the terrain. Through a curtain of whirling flakes, he spied a road winding below him and beyond that, at the bottom of a steep drop-off, was the lake that he would forever think of as Ava's.

Mack Dog erupted from the trees and skidded crazily to the road below before trotting around the corner. Luca shuffled carefully on his skis a few feet to the left which gave him a better view of the road below the hill on which he stood. He saw now where the dog was headed, to a battered pickup truck, the front driver's-side door open. Papers and an overturned cardboard box lay on the snow, as if thrown there along with a messy coil of rope and a toolbox with assorted wrenches scattered about.

He stood, mouth open as the man he knew as Uncle Paul burst out of the trees, cheeks flushed with exertion.

A second figure ran into view. Drawing close, she reached up a hand and stripped off her knit cap in irritation. The blond hair shone brilliant against the red of her jacket.

He did not hear what she said to her uncle nor did he need to. Ava Stanton, no longer an awkward teenager, stood just below him, like some strange memory come to life before his eyes. There was such intensity on her face, such rigidity in her body that his breath caught, nerves tingling.

As if she heard his thoughts, Ava tipped her head up.

Her blue eyes met his, widening, probably lost in the same incredulity he felt.

So riveted was he by those blazing eyes that he did not register the engine until a blue snowmobile appeared, the driver's face obscured by a helmet with a mirrored visor.

While Luca looked down at the bizarre scene, Paul's mouth rounded in shock. The machine roared closer.

Something odd and out of place appeared in the driver's hand, something black and shiny.

A gun.

Luca's pulse hammered.

No, not a gun, something different.

Luca's brain produced the fact even as his body pushed forward, hurtling down the icy hill as the snowmobile closed the gap to Ava and her uncle.

TWO

Ava tore her gaze away from Luca's face in time to see the snowmobile zooming toward them through a gap in the trees. She had no time to puzzle over Luca's sudden appearance. Feet frozen in shock, she felt the snow tremble under her boots, as the engine noise pierced the air with the intensity of a buzz saw. Ava had seen people do crazy things on the slopes before, something about the combination of speed and snow seemed to rob them of their senses, but this was different.

Her suspicions were confirmed when she saw something appear in the driver's left hand while his right still gripped the accelerator. It was squat, compact, unfamiliar, but her instincts screamed in fear. The machine closed in, and she shouted to her uncle.

"Uncle Paul!" Her words were lost in the scream of the engine.

Paul raised an arm to his head as if to ward off a blow, Mack Dog barking wildly at the approaching threat, unsure whether to make for his master or the oncoming mechanical monster.

Ava started forward with no better plan than to somehow get to her uncle. Her feet slipped and slid on patches of ice as she stumbled toward him. The snowmobiler was not more than fifteen feet away and closing rapidly, the black instrument aimed at her uncle. She saw that the hand gripping the weapon was ungloved, the finger now flipped up a trigger guard and pressed an illuminated button. Tiny projectiles exploded from the barrel. She watched in horror as they pierced Uncle Paul's jacket like a swarm of enraged hornets.

A wave of unseen energy swept through him. His body tensed and twitched as he went down, unconscious on the snow.

"No," Ava screamed, scrambling to get to him.

The snowmobile stopped just long enough for the driver to haul Paul's unconscious body up across his knees, and then the machine lurched forward again, heading straight for Ava.

Her blood turned to ice.

"You're not taking him," she yelled. "I won't let you."

She had no idea how to stop the assailant. The only notion that thundered through her mind was to somehow slow the person who was going to take away her uncle.

Her body went rigid, bracing for impact as the snowmobile's skis flew across the ground.

The mirrored visor reflected her terrified face back at her as the driver made the final approach.

She threw up her arms and screamed.

The air was knocked out of her as she was tossed aside, not by the impact of the snowmobile, but by Luca's body as he crashed into her and sent her sailing into a pile of loose snow. They fell in a tangle of skis and ice particles.

She felt his arms around her, trying to pull her away from the road, but she fought him off in spite of his strength.

"Let go."

His green eyes flashed behind the swirl of snow. "Stay down."

"Get off, Luca." She struggled to her feet and pulled herself free from him and the pile of snow, ignoring his clasping hands. Then she was running, following the ruts of the snowmobile, pushing as fast as she could against the wind.

"Uncle Paul," she screamed. Mack Dog raced along behind her, barking.

She heard Luca snapping off his skis, getting to his feet, calling out to her.

She ran up the hill and down toward the lake.

The snowmobile was stopped there, idling, the unconscious Paul still lying brokenly across the driver's lap. She could see the driver considering how to get by her car which was partially blocking the road. Going around would put the machine on unstable ice, possibly causing the skis to founder.

The other side backed to a steep incline covered with loose powder which would undoubtedly ensnare the machine in moments. Ava continued to run as fast as her complaining muscles would allow. His indecision gave her a slim chance. If she could get her uncle off the machine and into the car…

She closed the gap, ten yards, now five.

Reaching forward, lungs burning with the effort, her fingers strained to grasp the metal passenger grip.

Paul stirred, and she thought she could hear him groan.

Almost there. Almost.

As her fingers touched the cold metal of the passenger grip, the driver jerked into action, revving the motor. The snowmobile leaped forward into the pitched snow. For a moment, she thought he would not make it as the skis began to sink into the surface. With a surge of her last bit of energy, she grabbed the bar, clinging there as she was dragged along behind. Her weight unbalanced the machine and it slowed.

She'd done it. He would have to stop.

Then the snowmobile jerked and skidded, throwing her loose and sending her tumbling down the slope toward the lake.

Arms spread, hands clawing, she tried to stop her momentum. Sky blurred with snow as she tumbled toward the glittering oval bowl.

In dizzying glimpses she saw the driver wrestle the machine back up to the road and disappear into the distance as the lake rushed up to meet her.

Luca finally struggled clear of the snow. He'd seen enough to know that Paul had just been abducted although he did not give himself time to mull over the insane scenario. He texted an SOS with his GPS coordinates quickly to his sister.

She would send help. He took off in the direction the snowmobile had gone, a frantic Ava charging after it.

Doing his best to avoid the slick patches of icy snow, he ran as quickly as he dared until he slid close enough to witness Ava clinging to the back of the snowmobile. He saw her tensed fingers lose their grip on the bar as the machine bucked on the uneven snow. The unconscious body of her uncle Paul would have slipped to the ground as well if it weren't wedged under the handlebars.

The driver gave only a cursory look behind him as he fled onward, kicking up a cloud of white in his wake, Mack Dog in loud pursuit. Luca had no thought of giving chase as he scrambled to the edge of the slope where he saw Ava rolling helplessly, like a tumbling rag doll. He crashed down the hill after her, trying to calculate in his mind how it would end.

Would she stop before she reached the edge of the lake?

He remembered his early days apprenticing on a

Life Flight helicopter. The horrifying call on that crisp February morning; a child wandered out on the ice, fallen through. A father heedless of his own safety following his boy into the same deadly snare. That day it had switched from a rescue to a recovery and the anguish of it clung to him even after so many years. Luca blinked away the thought.

Ava would stop her desperate roll before she got to the water; she had to. He floundered through a deep pocket of snow, the cold seeping into his clothing and making his eyes tear. He flailed out of the depression in time to see Ava's jacket snag on a root thrust through the winter ice.

Her head bounced against the ground as she came to a stop, jacket precariously held in place by the small piece of wood.

Luca muttered a prayer of heartfelt thanks as his mind ran through options. Poised as she was only six feet above the lake, he would be able to reach her and drag her back up hill. The farther away from the water, the better.

Heart still pounding with exertion and adrenaline, he saw her eyes fixed on his.

"My uncle," she called to him. "I'm okay. Go help him. Please."

His heart skipped a beat at the raw emotion in her face. "Help is coming," he said, easing toward her down the slope. He placed each boot with care, trying not to dislodge the crusts of snow that might knock her loose from her perch.

"Luca, please go after Uncle Paul." She was nearly shouting now, tears trickling from her eyes and etching her face in frozen trails. "I'll climb back up in a minute. As soon as I get my breath. Please."

She was begging. He could not stand it. He spoke soothingly, a tone borne of many harrowing experiences in the fire service. "We'll get you away from the water. Then we'll find your uncle."

Her answer was lost in a churning of snow as Mack Dog appeared at the edge of the road where the snowmobile had made its risky maneuver around the car. When he caught sight of them down below, his tail began to whisk in excited circles and he charged down to meet them.

"Stay, dog, for once in your life," Luca thundered.

The dog paid no heed, pulling even with him. Luca reached out a hand to grab the jingling collar. Mack Dog moved toward Luca until he caught sight of Ava down below. He abruptly turned and plowed toward her, throwing frozen bits into the air.

"No, Mack Dog. Come here," Luca tried again.

Mack Dog trotted downslope and shoved his face into Ava's, nose first. She jerked back in surprise and the tiny movement was enough. The twig on which her jacket was snagged gave way and Ava slid like a human toboggan toward the lake.

"Luca," she screamed, her fear magnified by the thin air as she slipped away from him.

All thoughts of caution were gone now as he foundered down the slope, stumbling and falling as he went. At one point he was almost close enough to grab her, his fingertips grazing the slippery fabric of her jacket.

It wasn't enough. She skidded right through the scant black shrubs that protruded through the frozen layer at the water's edge and sailed out onto the iced surface of the lake, finally coming to a stop about ten feet out. Mack Dog started to follow her, but Luca grabbed his collar and yanked him to a sitting position.

"Stay."

Something in Luca's ferocious tone convinced the dog, and he sat obediently on the snow.

"Ava?" Luca called. For an agonizing moment, she lay still on the ice.

"Ava," he called again. "Look at me."

Slowly she raised her head, and his heart resumed beating. The ice held and she was conscious.

"Listen," he said. "You have to stay completely still."

She nodded and he put a tentative foot out on the ice. There was an ominous crack, loud as a gunshot. He stepped quickly back and checked his watch. He estimated the time he'd texted Stephanie to be about ten minutes ago. Help would be arriving soon, but he could not count on it. He looked around for a stick long enough to reach out to her and found nothing.

His mind flashed back to the contents of Uncle Paul's truck and the long tangled rope thrown out upon the snow.

"I'm too heavy to walk out to you. I'm going to go get a rope," he yelled to her. "Don't move until I get back."

She didn't answer, instead laying her head down on her arm.

The motion caused his heart to pulse with a mixture of emotions he could not decipher.

He wondered as he struggled up the hill, Mack Dog behind him, if she was thinking of her mother then. Luca suppressed a surge of anger at the woman who had cut Ava's heart to ribbons. How could anyone kill themselves and leave a vulnerable teen behind?

His muscles protested as he cleared the slope and ran up the iced road. He wanted to take out his phone and reassure himself that Stephanie was on the way but he could not do it, so strong was the rising tension inside him. Ava was petite. He could recall with ridiculous clarity how her slender wrist fit easily in the circle of his fingers when they would conduct arm wrestling contests. Delicate, but so was the ice that was the last barricade between her and a slow death by drowning.

He was sprinting now, the snow increasing from trickles to torrents, obscuring his vision momentarily as he paused to wipe his eyes. The truck swam into view, drifts of snow collected across the bed and partially concealing the contents strewn on the ground. He found the trail of rope, its end poking up just enough for him to grab hold. As he pulled it up, he noticed tiny metallic circles, like bits of confetti, slowly being swallowed up by the falling snow. He snatched one up and stowed it in his pocket before taking a quick look in the truck.

As he'd suspected. No keys, but he did find a leash which he clipped on the excited Mack Dog.

They took off running back to the lake, both Luca and the dog alternately stumbling on the slick ground. He tied Mack Dog to the fender of Ava's car, eliciting a bark of outrage.

"Sorry, can't have you adding any weight to the ice." He raced to the edge of the slope, immensely relieved to see Ava still lying there.

"I'm coming down," he called.

She didn't move.

Quickly he tied the rope around the sturdy trunk of a pine that stood sentry over the valley below. He unrolled it as he plunged back down the slope, praying it would be long enough to reach her. He made it to the water's edge with a good fifteen feet to spare.

Enough.

Barely.

"I'm going to throw you the rope. Grab an end and I'll haul you in."

No answer.

"Ava," he shouted, startling a bird in the nearby shrubs. "You've got to get the rope."

With no response from her, the feeling of dread in his gut increased. He knew that head injuries were silent killers. Her progress down the hill had been bumpy. Pulling his phone out with fingers gone numb from the biting cold, he saw the message.

SOS rec'd. 911 en route.

Stephanie didn't waste time asking superfluous questions. She was on her way with the ski patrol, he was sure.

But how long?

The snow was falling fast now. Ava's jacket was already covered in powder, flakes plastering her hair. How long before her body became hypothermic? "Ava, wake up," he shouted again, his strident tone ringing across the ice.

Something in her unconscious brain must have heard him, because she stirred.

"That's it," he called again. "Wake up. Open your eyes. I'm going to throw you the rope."

She raised her head, expression confused.

Breathing hard, he forced his tone from commanding to something calmer. "Here," he said. "I'm right here. You need to reach out your hand and get the rope, okay?"

She blinked and her blue eyes rapidly widened, a look of panic setting in.

Two seconds later he figured out why as the ice under her body broke, sending out splintering cracks in all directions.

THREE

Ava's stomach lurched in terror as she felt her legs drop through the ice and into the frigid water below. The breath was driven from her lungs. She'd thought she was numb from lying there for so long, but the cold was like an electric shock, jolting her body to the core. Arms scrambling, she tried to grab on to something, but her fingers raked through loose snow without finding a handhold. Inexorably she was sliding toward the exposed depths of the lake. Her feet splashed into the water.

"Luca," she screamed.

His body stiffened, mouth open.

Nothing she did slowed her progress. Just before her torso slipped in, she managed to hook her hands into a crack, holding the frozen mass to her body like a bizarre icy life preserver. Her legs remained submerged, but her head and shoulders were above water, at least for the moment.

Luca was shouting something, but the thundering of her heart drowned out his cries. She felt as if the lake was some live thing, sucking her down to the bottom, like it had done to her mother. In a few moments, her body would be claimed by it.

Ava felt the spark of anger light in her belly. Her mother had willingly offered herself up to death, walked into those dark waters and left her sixteen-year-old daughter behind with only an unpredictable uncle and a wounded father to care for her. She chose the lake, she chose her own drowning.

Why? Ava felt the puzzle rise again in spite of the horror of her situation.

Her mind circled the question that she'd wondered about countless times before.

Why did you choose these frigid waters over me?

Ava felt that old pain lance through her, through her frozen legs and into her heart, right up to her fingertips which were rapidly becoming too numb to maintain their grip.

I won't give up.

Ever.

I won't make the same choice you did, Mom.

She tried to hug the ice more tightly, but the strength seemed to be leaching out into the water that surrounded her. She kicked her legs to keep the circulation going, but they felt like two pieces of wood.

Luca tossed something at her. A rope, she finally realized. A spark of hope thrilled inside her as it slithered across the ice.

She tried to grab for it, but the motion almost

cost her her grip on the ice. The rope fell away and disappeared into the water between two floating pieces. She did not dare let go of the ice to fish around for it.

"I can't," she said, breathless.

"Yes, you can," Luca shouted, enraged. He reeled in the coil and tried again.

The rope hit the water just in front of her, splashing her face with stinging droplets. Blinking, she tried again to grab for it. This time the ice broke into several smaller pieces like a frozen jigsaw puzzle. She struggled to keep her grip on the larger of the chunks. Clinging there, breath coming in desperate pants, her body shivered violently.

Luca was furiously gathering in the rope, getting ready to toss it again. She saw him swinging the rope, strong arm tense.

"I can't get it, Luca," she called. "I can't let go."

She couldn't tell if he heard her or not. Despair added weight to her sodden clothes and she felt herself sinking lower into the water. Luca dropped his arm and turned away.

She felt oddly relieved. She did not want him to see her desperation, the fear that made her weak. Help would come soon, she knew. The ski patrol would make it on scene quickly enough, but hypothermia would arrive before they did. It could take less than fifteen minutes in freezing water for death to come. She clung tighter to the ice, trying to calculate how long she'd been in the grip of the frozen lake. Her arms were clumsy, fingers nearly useless.

Her gaze went to the road, to the rut marks left by the snowmobile. Who would want to hurt Uncle Paul? Truthfully, many. He'd crossed a number of people, cheated them even. There were plenty of men eager to settle a score.

She heard a noise and saw Luca with a rope tied around his waist, charging out onto the ice. Blinking to be sure she wasn't hallucinating, she looked again. What was he thinking? His six-foot muscled bulk would break through the ice in a moment and send him into the frozen water right along with her.

"No, Luca," she called, voice weak as a kitten's.

He did not alter course, so she tried to yell louder.

"Go back." Her words were faint but noisy thoughts crowded her mind.

Go back, Luca. Don't throw away your life for mine.

She felt sick at the thought, but she knew he would probably do the same for any other man, woman or child he found in the same situation, and probably an animal, too. She remembered the bird he'd told her about that he'd retrieved after it had gotten tangled in some old tree netting. People said he was crazy to climb a fifteen-foot pine to free a sparrow. People were right.

With dread, she watched him step onto the slick surface. Ice crackled around her as he planted one foot in front of the other, as if he was navigating some strange tightrope through the water. He moved closer, teetering slightly as he kept his balance. Face fixed in concentration, he moved slowly toward her until he was close enough for her to hear him.

"Hold on, Ava. I'll be there in a minute."

"Please go back," she whispered. *Please.*

She watched through blurry eyes as he stepped onto the chunk of ice near her, amazed that he had not fallen through. Her body shivered so badly she could hardly keep him in her field of vision.

Slowly, kneeling on a shelf of ice, he crouched over to grab for her sleeve. The green of his eyes was the only thing she could see clearly, just as vibrantly green as she remembered. His fingers gripped her wrist and she imagined they must be warm, warmer than hers anyway, but she could not feel anything. She was having a hard time seeing him through her growing cloud of confusion.

"Let go now, Ava."

She could not force her fingers to relinquish their grip.

Hold on, her mind screamed and her body obeyed, clinging in manic determination to that small hunk of ice.

"Let go," Luca demanded again.

She closed her eyes and pressed harder against the ice chunk, her limbs like the twisted branches of the trees that ringed Melody Lake.

His grip tightened around her wrist and he began

to pry her fingers away from the ice. "Ava, you're coming with me one way or another."

She was tired, more tired than she'd ever been. Her body felt suddenly as if it was heating up, warming from the inside. If she didn't get her jacket off, she thought she would roast.

She wiggled on the ice.

"What are you doing?" Luca said.

"Taking off my jacket. Too hot."

He grabbed both wrists now. "That's the hypothermia talking. You're not hot. You're cold and we're getting out of here."

He hauled her toward him, her legs sliding out of the water.

Her mind whirled from the sudden movement and she closed her eyes to steady herself. When she opened them again, she was looking into Luca's grave face. He was pulling her up, grabbing on to the front of her jacket, until she felt herself hoisted over his shoulder. She wanted to say something, to force her body to work in some way, but she could not. She found herself slung head down, staring at the milky ice beneath Luca's feet.

There was a sudden lurch, a cry of surprise from Luca and then the view changed as they both plunged through the ice.

Luca had the presence of mind to hold his breath when they broke through the crust and splashed into the lake. Frigid water enveloped him and he fought the urge to gasp at the pain of it. Holding as tightly to Ava as he dared, he kicked back to the surface. Shaking water from his eyes he turned her, his arms under her shoulders in the only maneuver that came back to him from his days as a high school lifeguard.

He heard her whimper softly, and the sound gave him renewed courage. There was still life in her, that tenacious spark that would be enough to help her survive this. Fighting against the shudders that shook his body, he freed one hand to find the rope he'd tied around his waist.

He tugged them along, one-handed. Their progress was a series of awkward, lurching moves that brought them incrementally toward shore. Broken ice floated around them, and he did his best to avoid the sharp edges, although he felt something cut into his arm anyway. His biggest concern was his hold on Ava which was weakening as the glacial water robbed him of feeling in his extremities.

The distance to the shore was probably only ten feet, but it may as well have been miles. At first Ava had tried to help, leaning into him and kicking feebly at the sharp bits of ice that crowded them. As time wore on, she had grown progressively more still until she was a deadweight.

"Almost there," he said. "Stay with me." He squeezed her as tightly as he could, his arm sinking into the pillowy layer of her jacket.

He pulled them both along, every movement an

agony. Slower and slower they moved until his hand slipped off the rope. Fear clawed at his insides as he struggled to keep Ava from floating away while he flailed for the rope.

His fingers would not cooperate. Clumsily he floundered, trying to force his hand to clasp the slick rope again.

Come on, Luca.

Grab it.

He felt his hold on Ava loosening. His choice came down to letting go of her or holding on and giving up on the rope, their only chance. He threw up a silent prayer, channeling his remaining stamina into keeping Ava in his arms.

Vision blurring, he looked in desperation at the shore which seemed to be miles away. Faintly he heard Mack Dog barking excitedly. Dark shadows swam in front of his eyes, and his ears began to play tricks on him. From far away he heard an engine approaching up the road at top speed. He imagined his sister roaring up in typical wild fashion behind the wheel of her Mustang.

It was imagination, purely. The logical side of his brain knew a car could never travel at such speeds on iced-over roads. Unable to muster the strength to attempt a one-armed swim stroke, he could only float, trying to keep Ava's chin above water.

"Luca."

The voice came from far away.

A woman's voice.

"Luca," the voice came again, louder.

He forced his eyes to focus on the face of his sister waving frantically, a snowmobile parked crookedly nearby. Someone was with her, a man wearing the red-and-black jacket emblazoned with the white cross of the ski patrol. There was a jerk on the line, and he was pulled toward the shore. All he had to do was hold tight to Ava.

It's almost over.

He forced himself to repeat it, although his body was frozen to a state of near agony. Ava's eyes were closed now, the white circle of her face just clear of the water, sections of hair floating like a corona in the dark water.

Almost there.

Tate, Stephanie's husband, pulled up on another snowmobile and hustled to the water's edge to meet them, his stiff leg making him ungainly.

They were close enough for Luca to see the ski patrol guy tugging madly on the rope, Stephanie assisting. In excruciating increments, they finally drew near enough for hands to grab hold of Ava and haul her out of the water. Tate and Stephanie each took one of Luca's frozen arms and dragged him out, too, immediately enveloping him in a thin, silver blanket.

"She was in the water longer than me," Luca said, through chattering teeth.

The ski patrol worker wrapped her securely,

strapping her into a toboggan. "We'll get her to the ambulance. It's just down the hill."

"Land a chopper," Luca choked out. "She needs to get to a hospital now."

"Snow movement near the landing site. Can't get a chopper in here. We're working on another accident and too much activity during avalanche conditions is a bad idea." The rescue worker didn't slow as he strapped Ava in and called into his radio. "Transporting now. I'll be there in five." He looked at Luca. "There's another ski patrol right behind me to take you."

Luca was too cold to answer.

Stephanie chafed his hands. "I got your SOS and called Tate. A guy at the lodge loaned me a snowmobile. I found the truck down the road, so I figured there was an accident. What happened?"

"Ava's Uncle Paul. Abducted."

Her eyebrows shot up. "Here? On the slopes? How did that happen?"

"Snowmobiler shot him with a Taser."

Luca noted a grave look steal over Tate's face. "Blue snowmobile?"

Luca nodded.

Ava moaned. In spite of Stephanie's restraining hand, Luca crawled over to her, his legs too weak to support him.

Her lips were a bluish tint, stark against the milky pallor of her face. She mouthed the words *Uncle Paul.*

He squeezed her hand with his own frozen fingers. "We'll find him."

Tate's frowned deepened.

"What is it, Tate?" Luca said as the ski patroller readied himself to pull the toboggan away.

Tate hesitated. "I was late because there's a rescue going on a few miles down the road from here. I had to go around."

Luca's stomach tightened.

"A rescue?"

Tate nodded, lowering his voice. "A snowmobile at the bottom of the ravine. Burned pretty bad. They figure it exploded on impact."

Luca forced out the words. "Blue?"

He didn't need to hear Tate's answer. He looked down at Ava and knew she'd heard it loud and clear.

A single tear fell, freezing a trail of grief onto her face.

Whoever had abducted Uncle Paul had probably caused his death, too.

Snow began to fall heavily now, and he brushed it away from Ava's cheek. The tips of his fingers were too cold to feel her skin, but it looked soft, feather soft.

A brisk breeze kicked up the snow around him, hissing as if it whispered secrets.

With a tingle of fear, he wondered if Ava would be the next life claimed on this rugged mountain.

FOUR

Sergeant Cecil Towers stood politely next to the bed, his dark eyes nearly a match for his dusky skin. His uniform was smartly pressed, fitting his slender frame nicely. A tinge of gray showed on his close-cropped hair. He reached out a hand to straighten the box of tissue on her bedside tray.

Her body reacted viscerally, edging away from the man who was guilty of nothing but informing her three weeks from the end of her senior year of high school that her mother's body had been recovered from Melody Lake. Even with her eyes closed she would never forget the tiniest detail of that visit, from the curve of his thin lips to his spotless uniform and the way he wiped his feet meticulously on the doormat before he'd entered Whisper Mountain Lodge.

Ava had gotten the gist of her situation from the nurses. She'd been more or less out for ten hours. No, she had not lost any fingers or toes amazingly, and no, they knew nothing about her uncle Paul.

She remembered Luca being there and although she'd willed herself to ask him, to beg him to tell her of her uncle, her body would not come out of its frozen stupor. Now there was no sign of Luca, but now she had a cop to pump for information.

"Are the police looking for my uncle?"

The question seemed to startle Towers, who raised an eyebrow and leaned closer. "Hello, there. I thought you were asleep, Ms. Stanton."

She repeated her question.

"First off, I'll tell you that we have not found your uncle. Why don't you go over the whole series of events? I was already briefed by Luca Gage, but let's see if you have anything fresh to add."

She told him every detail.

The Sergeant wrote with precision on a small tablet. When she ran out of words he smiled, revealing a chipped front tooth. "Did your uncle tell you about anyone who might have wished him harm?"

She shook her head.

He eyed her closely. "But there are people, aren't there? A long list, as a matter of fact, from disappointed investors, loan sharks…" He flipped back to an earlier page. "Disgruntled husbands."

Ava felt her face grow hot. "He wasn't perfect, but he deserves to be found, doesn't he?"

"Of course. We'll start a thorough background to come up with a list. In the meantime, we've got a crew up on the mountain searching." He slid his pencil back into his breast pocket. "You should know," he said, voice soft. "There has been a lot of snow movement where the machine went over, Ms. Stanton. It may be some time before we can locate the driver or anyone else."

Ava felt the walls crush in around her. She swallowed hard. "Are you saying if he's down there, hurt or dying you can't do anything about it?"

He sighed, as if he had been expecting the question. "The dogs are out and Search and Rescue, but the snow is continuing to move and the ravine is extremely deep. There's a storm coming in." He patted her hand where it lay on the bed, his palm oddly cool. "We'll do what we can, I promise."

Tears fell hotly down her cheeks. "He found something, some sort of treasure, and he was abducted. He's still alive, I know he is. You're not doing enough to find him."

The officer's eyes hardened for a moment. "Actually, I'm quite eager to take custody of your uncle. He's the reason I lost part of my front tooth last week."

Her mouth fell open. She was vaguely aware of Luca standing in the doorway, but she was too dumbfounded to pay him much heed. "My uncle broke your tooth?"

"To be fair, I walked into a dispute between your uncle and a local here in town. The local was extremely angry and threw an ashtray which intercepted my tooth instead of your uncle's face, although he deserved it more, no doubt." Another ghost of a smile that left no warmth in his eyes.

Ava groaned. "What did my uncle do this time?"

"Seems he sold the gentleman a necklace claiming it was an expensive antique." Sergeant Towers raised an eyebrow. "It was more along the lines of cheap costume jewelry. Of course the local was booked for assault, but by the time I'd sorted that out, your uncle had already taken off." The slight smile didn't leave his face. "So you see, if your uncle is still alive, I'm looking forward to speaking with him."

Towers wished her a good afternoon and promised to contact her soon before he left. Ava bit her lip. Uncle Paul's sins were catching up with him. Or was he already dead? Buried under a ton of snow and ice until the spring would release his body?

Through blurry eyes she saw Luca approach the bed. He was no longer the rambunctious teen she'd known. His shoulders were now impossibly broad, face filled out and the shadow of a beard showing on his unshaven face. How could he look so strong, so healthy in that all-American way as if he hadn't nearly drowned along with her? Someone had supplied him with dry jeans that clung to his long legs and a T-shirt that was too tight for his biceps. She swiped at her eyes with the sheet.

Luca stared at her, eyes wandering over her bruised face. "How are you feeling?"

"How am I feeling? How would you be feeling if

it was your uncle?" She clamped her lips together, mortified. *I'm sorry, I'm sorry,* she wanted to say, but she could not summon up the strength to make herself say it.

His cheeks colored slightly, the only reaction. "Right. Dumb question. Sorry. Let's stick to business, then. I've done some checking around. Your uncle didn't make many friends here. He was looking for something, following the trail of a wealthy man who used to live up the mountain."

She looked Luca over more closely, noting a bruise that darkened his cheekbone. He had no business walking out on that frozen lake to get her. She should be gracious, express her thanks. Instead, she wished with all her heart that he would go away and take his calm "I'm in charge" attitude with him. Now, above all things, she did not need him around, this wealthy successful man who made her stomach jump for some strange reason.

He continued to regard her with a contemplative look. "You said your uncle thought he found a treasure. What was it?"

"I don't know."

"He didn't give you any idea? Coins? Old stock certificates? Did he mention anything like that?"

"I said I don't know."

He thought for a moment. "We have to find out. It will lead us to whoever did this."

She gritted her teeth. "Look, I know you hunt for treasure professionally now, but…"

He suddenly flashed her a mischievous grin. "My exploits have reached even this humble hamlet?"

Her cheeks burned at the slip. So she'd kept tabs on his career. Who wouldn't? It was just an occasional internet search on an old high school friend. No, an acquaintance. She knew about the Gage siblings and their treasure hunting business that had recovered numerous rich prizes for private clients. But she had no intention of allowing him to become involved in her current mess. "You've done enough." She swallowed hard. "Thank you for getting me out of the water." She kept her eyes riveted to the faded Smokey the Bear on the front of his shirt. "I'll find out what happened to him on my own."

"How?"

"I'll hire someone. A detective."

Luca cocked his head. "It just so happens that Treasure Seekers is setting up a temporary satellite office right here in town until Uncle Paul's situation is resolved. Stephanie and Tate are already hard at work. Victor promises to join us when he can."

"No." She shook her head, sending a pain shooting up her neck. "You have a business to run." *No doubt a girlfriend waiting in San Francisco.* "I don't want you involved."

His smile was gentle. "I already am."

"You're not. You should leave."

He folded his arms, brows drawn together. "I

almost didn't make it out of that lake, either. That's something I take personally. Whatever your uncle found, someone was willing to kill you to get their hands on it. Maybe it's not a treasure, but then again, maybe it is."

She closed her eyes. "No, Luca. I don't want your help." When she opened them again, he was staring at her.

He sighed. "All right. Cards on the table. I have another reason for staying. I got a call from your father."

She stiffened. "Is he…"

"He's fine. The police called him to notify him about your accident. Because he couldn't talk to you, he called my father."

She should have known. Bruce had been friends with Wyatt Gage since their days serving together in Vietnam.

"He said to tell you he'll come as soon as he's fit to travel."

Ava groaned. She did not want her father on a plane so soon after a surgery to relieve pressure on his lower back. She'd just returned from visiting him. "I'll call him. Tell him I'm okay."

Luca nodded. "The doctors filled him in. He asked me to look into the situation, to find out what happened to your uncle and what he was after because he thinks it might endanger you."

She felt like screaming. "He can't stand Uncle Paul. He just wants him out of my life."

Luca appeared unsure how to respond.

"My uncle was looking for something, some sort of treasure. All I know is he was planning to buy an unclaimed storage unit. He told me a while back that he thought it might have belonged to a rich family, I think the name was Danson, but I don't know anything else, okay?"

"Okay. That's a place to start."

She drew herself up as high as she could against the pillows. "I don't want help. I can take care of myself."

He grinned. "That much I already know. I remember how you could make it down the mountain no matter how rough the snow or how bad the weather. You beat me every time we raced, and that bugged me like nobody's business."

She felt a small thrill that he remembered their time together as vividly as she did. "Proves my point," she said.

He bent slightly so he could look her full in the face and her stomach fluttered just like it had in high school when she drew near the popular, easygoing Luca Gage.

"Your father and my father go way back," Luca was saying. "He's asked me to look into this matter. I'm going to find a treasure if there is one and figure out what happened to your uncle Paul, because that's what I do."

"So it doesn't matter what I want?" she demanded, sitting up higher against the pillows.

"No," he said, turning to the door and giving her a cheerful smile. "It doesn't."

Luca found his sister waiting in the lobby, drumming manicured fingers against the dark denim of her jeans.

He shrugged. "She's okay. No permanent damage."

Stephanie's lips curved. "And I'm guessing from the look on your face, she wants you to leave her alone?"

He didn't answer.

"And I'm also guessing you're not going to cooperate?"

He paced to the window. "This isn't about Ava. I gave my word to her father. We're going to find out if there really is a treasure. It's the only way to find the person who abducted Paul and sent us to the bottom of the lake."

She watched him pace the beige tiled floor. "Typically, that's the police's job, crime solving and all that."

"This time they're going to have help. What do you know about John Danson? Paul might have bought his unclaimed storage unit."

She raised an eyebrow. "Danson? I remember we came across that name in one of our cases way back. He was a bit of an eccentric, the sole survivor of a wealthy family, but mentally unstable. I read in the paper he died six months ago, leaving no heirs and not much of an inheritance because he donated the family fortune to charity over the years."

"Not all of it. I remember reading that there was one item in the Danson treasure trove, a particularly valuable one, that never turned up."

She stretched her slender arms over her head and yawned. "And you happen to think Paul found that particular item?"

"Ava said her uncle was after Danson's storage unit."

She stood and smoothed her leather jacket. "Luca, even though you're a big dope sometimes, I love you anyway, so I have to say, this is dangerous."

He grunted. "What's dangerous? It couldn't be worse than getting caught in a burning building."

She shivered, no doubt reliving the perils of their last treasure hunt for a stolen violin that almost cost both Stephanie and Tate their lives. He was sorry for his joke. Another stupid remark from big-mouth brother. "Hey, I'm sorry. Poor taste."

She waved a hand. "Not that kind of dangerous. The kind of danger that comes from getting involved in complicated family business. Bruce doesn't like Paul. Ava loves him. Is the truth going to make things better or worse?"

He turned away, gazing out the window into the piles of dirty snow churned up along the newly plowed road. "I don't know."

She came close and put a hand on his arm, voice

soft, her head barely reaching his shoulder. "And I remember how you used to show off for Ava. I always thought you had a thing for her."

"I showed off for all the girls, not just Ava." He gave her a squeeze. "This is professional. Treasure hunting only. That's all I'm here for."

Stephanie chewed her lip. "Did you tell her Dad is interested in buying Whisper?"

"No, that seemed like a little much for the moment. I'll tell her at a better time."

Something flickered in her eyes, but mercifully, she did not comment. "Because I know better than to argue when you have your jaw set like that, I'll work on the details. The first thing is to find a temporary space for Treasure Seekers. Gold Summit is booked solid for the next two weeks. I'm still looking for a place."

He nodded, relieved to be hammering out a plan. "Doesn't have to be fancy. An internet hookup, a couple of mattresses on the floor, and I'm fine."

"Speak for yourself. I require better accommodations than that, and it's gotta take dogs."

"Dogs?"

She nodded. "Until Ava is sprung and takes possession of Mack Dog, he's your new hairy little brother."

He laughed. "I always wanted another brother. Victor is no good at fetch."

"Swell, then you can share your mattress with

him. Tate filled up his pockets with dog biscuits and took him for a walk."

Pockets.

The word sizzled through him and he jerked. "I can't believe it."

"What?"

"Some investigator." He groaned. "I'm an idiot."

"Not all the time," Stephanie replied. "But what did you do this time?"

"It's not what I did, it's what I didn't do. I know how to find out who abducted Paul. The answer has been in my pocket the whole time." He jogged for the door.

"What?" Stephanie said. "What are you talking about?"

He didn't reply as he sprinted into the late-afternoon sunlight.

It was nearly noon the next day when Ava eased out of her car, her ribs and legs sore and complaining, tired from the effort of convincing the doctors to discharge her. Even though she'd wanted to head immediately to the spot where the police were concentrating their rescue efforts, she'd been clearly ordered in polite tones by Sergeant Towers to keep out of the way. He further informed her that the contents of Uncle Paul's truck had been seized and would be returned when the police were good and ready.

Didn't matter. Ava knew where Uncle Paul had

been staying to spearhead his ridiculous treasure hunt. It was a start anyway.

The Peak Season Trailer Park was as tidy as it had been for the last twenty years, nicely tended units with cement walkways between that were cleared of snow. Uncle Paul often stayed at the place over the years when he was avoiding facing Ava's father.

"Paul's a scammer and he always has been. Every time he shows up here he wants money for some ridiculous scheme," her father had said with increasing frequency in the months before a blown tire caused the wreck that paralyzed him.

Marcia, her mother, would not reply, dipping her head and chewing her lip. Ava knew what she was thinking then.

He's my brother. He needs my help.

The thought startled her, so like the words running through her own mind at that moment.

He's my uncle. He needs my help.

But now a grimmer thought chased right along behind.

If he's still alive.

He was her mother's only relative. If he was dead, wouldn't she feel it? Have some sense that his life had blinked out?

No, she acknowledged. She would not feel it. The place where her soul had been was sodden and numb. A nebulous hope was all she had left and she would hold on until it was pried from her cold fists.

Resolutely, she crunched through the snow to the caretaker's trailer.

A familiar man with ruddy cheeks and a crew cut prickling his big head greeted her. His jowls were fleshier than she remembered. His overall rumpled quality remained the same from the faded jeans to the tattered down vest he might have been wearing steadily since she'd seen him some ten years before.

"Ava Stanton, you're all grown up," he said, squeezing her in a hug that nearly made her cry out.

"Hello, Bully. Good to see you."

"You, too. Pauly told me you're a real looker, and I can see he's not joking." Bully's smile dimmed after a moment. "Uh, you know the cops have been here. Said he's in trouble. Said maybe he'd been abducted."

She told him what she knew.

Bully considered. "You think he's dead?"

She sighed. "I'm not sure."

His rounded shoulders slumped. "Ah, things finally caught up with Pauly."

Her heart sped up a tick. "What things?"

Bully looked away. "You know. Pauly's a scammer, no disrespect intended."

"But what was he involved in this time, Bully? Who was after him?"

"Dunno. He was scared about something. Told me not to tell anyone he was staying here." Bully's eyes narrowed. "Wouldn't even tell me what was up, and haven't I known the guy for twenty years?"

She felt an inexplicable thickening in her throat. "Don't let it get you down. He didn't tell me, either."

Bully's shrugged. "Heard you was going to sell Whisper Mountain."

She raised an eyebrow. "That's the plan. Did Uncle Paul tell you?"

"Naw, just heard it somewhere."

She wondered where, but she did not press the point.

Bully pulled a toothpick from the dispenser on his small table and chewed it. "Told Pauly I heard about the sale, and you know what he says to me?"

He leaned in close enough for her to catch the scent of bacon that clung to his flannel shirt.

Bully's brow wrinkled. "He tells me, 'Don't believe everything you hear,' and he flashes this smile like I-got-a-secret-that's-going-to-turn-things-up-side-down. What do you think that means?"

Ava could only shake her head. "I don't know, but I'm going to find out."

"Anything I can do to help?"

"I'll let you know if I think of anything."

"That's fine, then." Bully nodded and handed her a key. "He's staying in the one he always does, number 17. Some people came this morning and wanted to rent out a few trailers, but I ain't about to rent that one out even though the police have cleared it. No one is staying in that trailer 'cept you until we figure out what happened to Pauly."

Ava nodded, unable to speak, accepted another

crushing hug from Bully and followed him outside, shivering. Bully's puffy vest had a tear down the back, but the man seemed completely impervious to the temperature, as if he was showing her the way to some beachside cabana instead of a trailer parked in the snow. She trudged along the path to number 17, feeling the weight of the past twenty-four hours slowing her down.

What could she hope to discover in her uncle's trailer?

"Here you are," Bully announced grandly. "I just put a new microwave in not two months ago. Works slick as a whistle."

She thanked him again, grateful that he did not trap her in another rib-crushing hug before he left.

Sliding the key in the lock, a movement caught her eye. Someone looked out from the trailer that faced hers.

Someone familiar.

FIVE

Mack Dog pulled out of Luca's slack grip and bounded over to Ava.

Ava rubbed the dog's ears, but her eyes were on Luca as he leaned on the porch railing of trailer number 18, dead across from the one Ava had entered a moment before.

He should wave, give her a cocky smile as if she was an old pal meeting them by chance, but he found he could not. The look frozen onto her face stopped him, an expression that said she did not want him there. It was not a surprise, but he felt a twinge anyway.

I promised your father, Ava, he told himself, walking over to join her.

"What are you doing?" she demanded.

He went for calm and confident. "I told you we were setting up headquarters until we find out what treasure Paul was after. Did you think I was making it up?"

"No," she said.

He shifted. "I've got this trailer, and Stephanie and Tate have the next one." He braced himself for a fight, but she offered only a resigned shake of the head which disturbed his equilibrium. He remembered her as a scrappy teen who didn't back down from anything, and he liked her that way.

"You've got the right to stay anywhere you like. Do what you have to do. Thanks for keeping Mack Dog. I'll take care of him now."

She turned away and stomped up the steps, stopping to finger a pair of skis that nestled upright in the corner of the porch. Her fingers traced the edge gently, lovingly almost. He wondered how much skiing she had been able to do since she'd moved away. His brain dredged up indelible images of Ava flying like the swiftest of wild birds, on silver skis across snow so white it dazzled the vision.

"Before you go, something came up that might help." He watched her turn, the blue of her eyes vibrant in her pale face.

She stood silently, waiting, hands rammed into her pockets.

Luca thought he heard the crunch of footsteps from behind the trailers, or maybe it was the snow falling from the thickly clustered pines that ringed the park. He moved closer, dropping his volume. "Do you know anything about Tasers?"

She shook her head. "Not much other than they fire prongs that send an electric current into the—" she swallowed "—the victim."

"Yes. When a Taser is fired, it releases a bunch of tiny coded tags, little metal circles like confetti almost. The police can use the serial number on the tags to get a complete trace of the weapon including the person who purchased it."

Ava's brows shot up and she closed the gap between them. "Did the police find one of the tags?"

He cleared his throat. "No, the snow covered up the whole scene by the time they got there. But right after Paul was taken, I stuck one in my pocket. Somehow, it was still there even after our little adventure in the lake. I gave it to the cops this morning."

Her face lit up and she threw her arms around him. "So we'll know soon. We'll know who did it and why."

He held her close, her hair tickling his face. His hands wanted to explore her shoulder blades and skim the smooth skin on the back of her neck. Her small soft frame fit perfectly in his embrace before she pulled away and he returned to his senses.

The hope and longing in her face struck him dumb for a second. She still believed it was going to turn out all right for Paul, but he knew she was wrong. In typical Luca Gage fashion, he'd just made things worse, if that was even possible.

"They'll contact you when they know."

They lapsed into an awkward silence until Mack Dog's barking broke in. Luca and Ava turned toward the snow-covered trees behind the trailers.

Luca held up a hand and eased his way through the knee-deep drifts. He found himself in a quiet wood, still, except for the wagging tail of Mack Dog, who thrashed around, throwing up puffs of white. Mack Dog darted away, disappearing for a few moments before he trotted back, presenting himself to Luca, flakes clinging to his whiskers.

"What are you after?" Luca asked.

He was startled by Ava's voice at his side. "A rabbit or squirrel?"

"Probably." Luca wondered as he led the way back to the trailer door. "Mind if I take a look inside?"

Ava hesitated only for a moment before she unlocked the door and let them both in, Mack Dog barreling in behind them. He kept a careful distance this time and a firm hold on the reason for his mission.

The interior was old, the wood paneling worn and Formica-topped table dated. There was not much left in the trailer, and Luca knew the police had photographed everything and taken anything relevant to the investigation. All that remained was a sleeping bag rolled up on the bottom bunk, stacks of books cluttering the narrow counter and a well-gummed chew toy on the floor near the bed. A dirtied coffee cup and a half dozen stubby pencils with chewed erasers adorned a dusty shelf. Mack Dog had his own neatly folded blanket on the floor which he promptly flopped down on, curling himself into a semicircle.

Luca picked up a book and read off the title. "*Gemology, the Treasures Underneath.* Ironic."

"Why?" Ava said sharply. "Your sister is somewhat of a gemologist, isn't she? Lots of people have that hobby."

He tried for a patient tone. "We've been doing some research. Your uncle was looking for the Sunset Star. It was owned by John Danson before he died. It's a pearl, a 130-carat pink pearl to be precise."

He was astonished when her face crumpled and tears began to make trails down her cheeks. His mind raced. Woman crying. Should he offer a hug? A drink of water? Call someone? Finally, he moved toward her, but she held up a hand.

"Sorry." She shook her head. "The pearl, that horrible pearl. That's what he was always searching for."

Luca shook his head, relieved that she was speaking again. "I don't follow."

She took a shaky breath and wiped her face. "It was also his nickname for me. He said I was his 'pearl of great price.'"

Luca flashed on the parable. "Like the merchant looking for pearls. He finds the most precious one and sells everything he owns to obtain it."

"He's been looking for that pearl his whole life. The one big score that will make everything else pale in comparison. It's almost like a disease that's followed him for as long as I've known him. It would come and go, these quests of his, but after Mom died just before I graduated high school..." She began to pace in small circles on the worn tiled floor. "This time was different."

"Different, how?"

"He did it for me. Whatever this quest is that got him abducted and maybe...maybe killed. He was going to find that pearl so I wouldn't have to sell Whisper Mountain."

"But selling would make financial sense, wouldn't it?" Luca felt a twinge. "I thought you wanted to sell it." Should he tell her of his father's plans?

She shot him a look. "How did you know that? I didn't tell anyone. You seem to know all about my plans, and so does Bully."

"The guy who runs this place?"

"Yes."

Luca frowned. "So how did he find out? Did Paul tell him?"

"He says not." She fixed him with a hard stare. "How did you know, Luca?"

The old rotary phone shrilled, and Ava jumped, snatching it quickly off the cradle.

Luca was ashamed of his relief in dodging the question.

She pressed the phone to her ear. "Hello, who's there?" Luca came closer, so close his cheek nearly touched the smooth satin of hers. Feather soft, just like he'd imagined. *Knock it off, Luca.*

He blinked and listened in.

No one spoke.

Ava felt a chill creep up her spine. "Who is this? Who is calling?"

Luca took the phone from her hand. "Talk or we're hanging up."

The phone went dead, the dial tone sounding loud in the dead silence of the trailer.

A wrong number? Luca felt a tickle deep in the pit of his stomach. "Did you hear anything?"

"No. I thought it might be someone breathing at first, then nothing."

Luca's mind raced. Someone knew the phone number. There was nothing random about that call.

Stephanie and Tate appeared in the doorway. Luca joined them on the porch. Mack Dog leaped from his cushion and ran to Tate, poking his nose into Tate's shin.

Tate dropped stiffly to one knee and wrestled with the eager canine.

"I think he missed you," Stephanie said with a smile for her new husband.

"I guess I still smell like Milk-Bones."

Stephanie flashed a more subdued smile at Ava and Luca was struck by how different they looked, Ava, white-blonde with sapphire eyes and Stephanie, dark hair and chocolate eyes. There was something common to both, he thought. Determination shone clearly on each of their faces. Strong women. He wouldn't want it any other way.

Stephanie clasped Ava's hand. "Usually our clients seek us out and hire us to find their missing treasure. This is awkward, I know."

Ava nodded, chin high. "Awkward doesn't begin to describe it."

Tate exchanged a look with Luca as if to say, *How bad is this going to get?*

Luca shrugged. Two determined women. Who could say?

Ava chewed her lip. "What do you want to do?"

Stephanie's look was all business. "The police are trying to figure out who snatched your uncle. As treasure seekers, we're focused on the why. We're starting a search to trace John Danson's activities. His father owned a huge place up in the mountains until he died about ten years ago. Did your uncle mention anything about him?"

Ava sighed. "No. I hadn't spoken to Uncle Paul much in the last few months. I moved away, and he stayed on to look after Whisper Mountain, work on some investment opportunities as he called them."

"He met with a real estate agent six months ago," Stephanie said. "The same agent my father..."

Luca shot her a warning look, but she ignored him.

Ava quirked an eyebrow. "I didn't know that, but it makes sense. He finally realized hanging on to Whisper Mountain was a lost cause."

Stephanie cocked her head. "Could be, but that agent handled the sale of Danson's estate. I think Paul was tracking the pearl, trying to find out what happened to it."

Ava crossed her arms. "If you want to go hunt for a treasure, it's all yours. I don't really care about this pearl or whatever he was after. I've got other priorities."

Luca tried to rein in his flash of irritation. He was not in this thing for his own personal gain. "You may not care, but someone does. Find the treasure, and the truth comes out."

Checking her watch, she sighed. "My uncle is missing. I've got to go. I'll let you know if I hear anything that might help you find the pearl."

"Where are you going?" Luca called as she scooted by him out the door.

"Tate, can you take care of Mack Dog until I get back?" Ava tossed over her shoulder, ignoring Luca's question.

"Sure." The dog sat contentedly, tail swishing, at Tate's feet.

Luca stalked after her outside.

His feeling of unease grew as he saw her grab the skis from the porch as well as an old set of snowshoes and head for her car. She thought she could fix things herself, and she would listen to reason about as well as a bull charging for the red cape.

Let her go.

It's what she wants.

"Strong women," he grumped to himself, "can be a real pain." With an exasperated sigh, he grabbed his own spare skis and snowshoes off his own trailer porch and ran after her.

Before she got the car reversed down the walkway, Luca appeared behind the bumper making it impossible for her to leave without running him over. When she stopped, he joined his skis and snowshoes to hers in the back before climbing into the passenger seat, his big frame crammed into the small vehicle.

"It's a bad idea," he said. "Police are searching. They don't need civilians getting in the way."

She didn't bother to feign innocence. "I don't need your permission."

He huffed. "I wasn't trying to be your boss. I was trying to get you to see reason."

"Why is it that 'seeing reason' means agreeing with your viewpoint?"

"Because my viewpoint is correct." He clamped his mouth closed with an audible click.

Even though she kept her gaze riveted out the front window, she could feel his eyes on her face, the green of them glittering in her imagination. Those eyes, she'd spent many a teenaged daydream wishing those eyes would turn on her with admiration. "This would be easier if I went alone."

Luca buckled his seat belt. "I never do things the easy way. Just ask my brother and sister."

Because she could think of no reply and Luca was not going to budge from the passenger seat, she pulled onto the road heading for the ridge where the police were concentrating their search and rescue efforts.

Luca examined the terrain. "Going to be dark in a couple of hours. They'll suspend the search until morning."

Suspend the search. So businesslike. She kept her voice as level as she could manage. "You don't think he's alive anyway, do you? You think this is a recovery, not a rescue." She glanced at him in spite of herself. She wanted to see hope there, some glimmer that would keep her desperate desire alive. Instead, she saw the hard kernel of truth.

"Ava," he said quietly, "it's been more than twenty-three hours. There was a storm last night. There's another rolling in."

"Uncle Paul's a survivor," she snapped. "He's had wilderness training. He knows how to make a snow cave. He taught me when Dad was away on business." She was dismayed to hear her voice crack.

Luca put a hand out toward her shoulder, but he did not make contact. It was probably the stiffness in her posture that told him his touch was not welcome. She found she regretted his restraint, wondering what the stroke of his fingers on her skin would feel like. *Don't let him charm you. He's only here for treasure.*

She gritted her teeth and guided the car up the

mountain, finally pulling as close as she was able to the barricade the police had erected at the top of the ridge. She hadn't expected to get any closer. Climbing out she headed toward Sergeant Towers, who stood at the top of the slope, radio in hand, breath puffed white in the cold air.

He did not look surprised to see her. "Good afternoon, Ms. Stanton. Hello, Luca."

"What have you found?" Ava said, her eyes scanning the whitened ravine below.

"Some scorch marks indicate the snowmobile slid about twenty feet before it impacted a rock shelf and broke apart."

She swallowed hard, waiting.

"We've got people rappelling down to the bottom now, but there's been about a foot of new snow. The dogs can't get down there."

"Have they found my uncle?" she said, forcing the words out.

After what seemed an eternity, he answered, "No." He eyed the sky. "We're going to have to call it in about an hour."

"You can't," she said. "He's alive. I know it."

Sergeant Towers's calm demeanor did not change, but there might have been a softening in his dark eyes. "You were ski patrol. You know how it works. We can't risk the safety of our people. We'll start again first thing in the morning."

Ava wanted to scream. Instead, she bit her lip so hard she tasted blood.

Towers shot a look toward her car, noting the skis. "If you've got any ideas about searching on your own, don't. Unstable snow and darkness are a lethal combination."

"I know these slopes, and I know the dangers."

"Then you know I don't have the resources to conduct two rescues." Sergeant Towers spoke calmly, but the words had a whisper of steel in them.

"You're not in rescue mode. You're looking for bodies." She wished she hadn't said it, but the officer did not seem to take offense.

Luca stepped closer. "Did you get anything off the Taser tags?"

"Not yet. We've been busy and this is a small department, not like San Francisco." The sly dig was evident in spite of the pleasant inflection. Towers used binoculars to scan below where a rescuer in a yellow vest made his way down a spine of rocks that projected above the snow. The phone clipped to his belt beeped, and he excused himself to answer it.

Ava did not waste time. She headed back to the car. Luca had to jog to catch up.

She eased the car back down the trail until she came to a spot where she could manage a turn. The tires spurted snow as she guided the vehicle a half mile down the road, ignoring Luca's barrage of questions.

She drove up toward a rocky promontory, a

splayed section of granite cliff, broad and flat like a smooth, outstretched palm. She parked the car on the road and buckled on Uncle Paul's old snowshoes, her throat thickening unexpectedly as her fingers ran over the graceful ash frames and the rawhide lacing. Uncle Paul made the snowshoes himself as a teen, whiling away hours in the Maine woods.

"I'd give you the shirt off my back, Ava, but not my snowshoes," he'd say with that infectious grin.

Luca had paused a moment in between snapping on his high-tech aluminum snowshoes.

"I remember hearing about Uncle Paul's snowshoes from your father," he said softly. "Those the ones that almost sent Mack Dog to the pound?"

She smiled in spite of herself. "Yes. He chewed the rawhide webbing, and I've never seen Uncle Paul as mad as he was then. Mack Dog had to bunk in my room for three days until Uncle Paul forgave him."

Luca reached out a hand, his fingers grazing her own, momentarily bridging the chasm that separated them and sending a jolt of electricity through her bones. "You didn't buckle this one right."

"Thanks." She pulled her hand away, ignoring the tingling his touch left behind, and fixed the strap. "Let's go. The view from up there is the best vantage point," she said more to herself than him.

They waddled their way upslope, crunching over the snow. The air was so cold it made her eyes sting. Pines rustled above them. The sergeant was right. A storm was coming.

She increased her pace until she was breathing hard, ribs complaining and one knee beginning to stiffen. Months of teaching every available ski lesson and taking numerous shifts on ski patrol had gotten her no closer to saving Whisper Mountain, but it had taken a toll on her body. The near drowning had only added more pain to the load. She forced herself to move faster until Luca was panting in his effort to keep up.

Odd projections of granite protruded through the snow. A bird, feathers puffed against the breeze pecked among the rocks, oblivious to the snow which had begun to fall.

Ava crunched as close as she could to the edge of the rocky plateau until the scenery played out beneath her. She was struck by the beauty of it in spite of the fear that bubbled in her gut. How could she be witness to something so grand? A glittering landscape so beautiful it could only have been made by God Himself? It made an ache inside her for a moment, a longing she couldn't describe until darker thoughts took over.

God wasn't welcome in her world anymore.

She would not let Him back into her life. She would put Him away in that painful place inside her, boxed up with memories so anguished they must be contained so they would not cut her to shreds with their razor-sharp edges. She blew out a breath to clear her mind.

A nudge on her arm startled her out of her reverie.

Luca held a pair of binoculars out to her. "They were in the front seat of your car."

She scanned until she picked out the yellow vests of the search and rescue team. But it was not the ravine that drew her attention as much as the area spreading out along either side, a gentle ribbon of ground that hosted a trickling stream in the summer. Now it was frozen under piles of snow, shrouded by pine and fir trees.

If he was alive, Uncle Paul would make his way there, screened by trees and sheltered from the wind.

If he'd survived the crash.

If.

She'd never realized before how such a tiny word could hold such a world of hope wrapped up inside it.

If you're alive, I'll find you.

Ignoring the cold that had begun to seep through her jacket, Ava set off away from the promontory, into the curtain of falling snow.

SIX

Luca concentrated on keeping pace with Ava. He tried to push other thoughts from his mind, but they crowded in anyway. He'd flown over these mountains many times in his years of piloting a helicopter. Rugged terrain, made more inhospitable by winter conditions. He knew they would not find Uncle Paul alive. That left more grisly options to churn through his gut as they began the arduous descent.

The Sierras were home to black bears who, contrary to popular belief, did not fall into the dead sleep of hibernation. They emerged from their dens periodically and not in the most complacent of moods. He'd encountered one particularly angry female while backpacking with his brother. The mother bear did not appreciate their proximity to her sleeping cubs. Never underestimate the power of a determined female protecting her family. He shot a look at Ava and then the sky, estimating the temperature to be somewhere in the low teens. The previous night had similar temps, but with the wind chill and active snowfall, it would have been dangerous to be trapped outside, even for someone who hadn't recently been injured and abducted.

The list unrolled in his mind: shock, internal bleeding, exposure, hypothermia, head injury.

And an abductor ready to finish Paul off?

Where did that factor into the list? Nothing changed his earlier certainty that their mission would not have a happy ending. The best they could do would be to figure out who was after Paul's treasure. It would help her find closure, but there would not be a happy ending for Ava. He rolled his shoulders to ease a sudden pain in his chest.

She stopped so suddenly that he almost plowed into the back of her.

"I thought I heard something."

They both listened. He picked up what might have been a shout from far away, the direction where the rescuers were working. Now he detected only the rustle of the wind in the pine needles.

He did a slow half circle, taking in the green black pines and the dazzle of crystalline snow. A glint from a nearby ridge made him do a retake, but although he stared until his eyes burned, he could not see anything amiss.

Ava continued on, and he followed.

They'd been traveling for an hour since they'd strapped on the snowshoes, their trek keeping pace with the sun as it began its descent. He looked back up at the ridge where Ava's car was parked. The return trip would take twice as long. He'd have to stop her, and he didn't relish the thought.

You should end it now. This is futile, and you know it.

She had already moved forward into the thick screen of trees. He plodded after her pushing by branches and wiping the spray out of his eyes. They emerged on the frozen creek bed.

"Uncle Paul would have followed the creek to find a place to hole up that was sheltered from the wind." She scanned up and down. "There's plenty of snow here to make a cave and it's far enough away from where the snowmobile went over that he could escape the kidnapper."

She couldn't recognize the flaw in her own hopeful logic. If Paul survived the crash unscathed, the kidnapper would likely have, too, following right along behind. There would be no hiding from the guy, whoever he was.

Ava continued, undaunted. "He'd pick a spot with deep snow. The opening would face the leeward side to keep the wind out."

He checked the forecast on this phone. No change. The storm was still barreling toward them.

"Ava…"

"And there would be a ventilation hole if he had time to make one. Maybe he cut branches to lie on." She began to examine the pine trees, looking for broken twigs.

The snow fell harder as she continued to move farther away from their route out. He scanned the far side of the bank, keeping an eye on the clouds that now seemed to absorb the sunlight.

"Ava, we have to go back. We can't get caught here when that storm comes in."

"A few more minutes," she called, stopping at a dome of snow. He watched as she shoved a stick down into the bowl of white, hating the sad look on her face when she straightened. She'd have to face the truth. He wondered why the thought bothered him so much.

Flakes collected on her hat, spangling her hair. Her cheeks were pink, eyes glittering feverishly. "Maybe a little farther down. He could have made it that far."

She'd made it two more steps when he caught up, turning her to face him. His fingers easily encircled her wrist, so delicate.

"We've got to go back. I'm sorry."

She shook her head, sending snowflakes dancing back to the ground. "He might be out here."

He didn't let her look away this time, instead putting his hand to her cheek and directing her gaze to his. "He's not. He could not have made it this far from the crash site."

"But…"

He took hold of both her gloved hands and moved

her closer, feeling his heart thump unsteadily. "I'm sorry. I really am."

The air seemed to go out of her and she pulled her hands away, shoulders slumped.

After one last look down the frozen creek bed, she followed him back the way they had come.

He felt like he was somehow responsible. She was giving up. Would a few minutes more of searching have hurt? A couple more moments for her to decide for herself that it was time to go?

Uncertainty was not natural to him, and he wondered why this one small woman seemed to awaken it in him.

He was going for his phone, to check one more time to see if the storm had altered course, weakened somehow, when Ava let out a yelp and surged forward, moving faster in her snowshoes than he would have thought possible.

"What is it?" he yelled.

She didn't answer, just kept hurrying toward a tangle of trees up the bank.

He applied himself to following along, his own progress much more clumsy.

She charged through the falling snow which was now flowing in a silent curtain down on them. "I saw something. Right up here."

He struggled to keep up as she started up a snowbank.

"Something red," she puffed. "Uncle Paul was

wearing a red cap. I knew he came this way. I knew it."

Foreboding took root in Luca's gut as Ava shoved her hands into the shrubs, pushing aside the iced branches.

"I'll help," he said, stripping off his gloves, ignoring the frigid temperatures that bit at his skin. The sooner she ended the wild goose hunt the better.

He had only begun to paw through the branches when Ava let out a whoop of joy. She thrust out a hand and pulled out a bit of red cloth. "I..."

The triumph slowly faded away as she looked closer. It was a torn glove, one finger missing and unraveling at the bottom. It was a child's glove, no doubt left behind from a tobogganing adventure, the worn condition indicating it had been there for some time.

"I thought..." she began.

She did not cry. He wished she had. The disappointment and grief that filled her eyes was far worse. He could not tell if it was sorrow or the passing clouds that turned the iridescent blue irises dark and flat. In that moment he would have done anything, said anything to bring the spark back.

"I'm sorry" was all he could think to say.

She turned away quickly, too quickly, and her snowshoes got tangled underneath her. She fell on her knees, sinking down into the snow. He dragged her up again and for a moment, wrapped her in his arms, pressed his cheek to her forehead. She was fighting hard not to cry.

She whispered, voice ragged. "Luca, do you think my uncle is really dead?"

He held her there, willing comfort and warmth back into her frame at the same time his body relished the feel of her next to him. "The police will know soon."

She gathered herself then, the shutter falling into place, as she pulled out of his arms.

"We should go see if they've found anything."

He led the way this time, grateful that she could not see his worry. Ava was strong, strong enough to survive her mother's suicide, but it seemed the loss had piled a greater weight on her soul and darkened her spirit, blotting out the irrepressible joie de vivre he remembered. How would she survive this new blow?

It's not your problem, Luca. She made that clear. Ava wasn't his business, but his heart and body did not seem to be getting the message.

The clouds cast strange shadows on the snow as they made their awkward way back to the car. At the top, something made him pause and turn back to the frozen riverbed. He looked again for the strange gleam that he'd imagined earlier.

There was nothing but the howl of the quickening wind.

* * *

Ava stripped off the snowshoes and placed them carefully in the trunk. Uncle Paul's snowshoes, his pride and joy. Cold seemed to infuse her from the inside out. She'd been so sure she would find him. He would creep out from some cleverly constructed snow cave, flash that grin at her and they would face the challenge of selling Whisper Mountain together.

The wind murmured in her ears.

He's gone.

She fought an urge to scream into the sky.

Stop taking everything away.

I cannot endure any more pain.

"Stop," she whispered.

Luca looked up from the fender where he'd sat to remove his snowshoes. "What did you say?"

She had not realized she'd uttered it aloud. Tucked inside his words was an undercurrent so gentle that she did not trust herself to answer. The threads holding her heart together were fragile, like the strands of ice glazing the delicate pine needles above them. One shift, one gust of wind and they would shatter. Somehow instinct told her to keep Luca away, far away. She waved him off and headed toward the driver's seat.

He stopped her with a touch on her forearm. "Why don't I drive back?"

No energy to argue. No reason to resist. She handed him the keys.

He turned over the engine just as his phone rang.

"Hey, Stephanie. We're heading back now." Luca shot a quick glance at Ava. "No. Nothing to report." He listened intently for a moment before turning to her. "Do you know a Sue Agnoti? Her name sounds familiar."

Ava nodded. "She's been a caretaker at Whisper for years. We've been paying her and her husband a little to keep up the place. They live there now."

"She's been calling the trailer every few hours. She's coming to talk to you."

"Twenty-plus years ago she was Uncle Paul's girlfriend. That's how she came to Whisper in the first place." Ava heaved a sigh. "Uncle Paul messed things up of course, but they've been friends for decades anyway. What will she say when I tell her he's..." Ava clamped her mouth shut tight.

"I'll tell her, if you'd like me to."

"No, thank you. I'll do it."

"You also got a call from a Charlie Goren, a friend of your uncle."

"I don't know him, but at least someone thinks of Uncle Paul as a friend."

Ava tuned out as Luca finished the conversation with Stephanie. He guided the car back toward the main road, making it only a few feet when the text from Sergeant Towers came in.

Luca stopped the car to read from the screen. "They're suspending the search until morning," he told her.

She nodded, leaning her head back against the seat, eyes turned toward the ridgeline. Was he lying there now? Buried under an immovable mass of ice? Had he suffered?

Imagination began to play cruel havoc. Many a time she had wondered if her mother had suffered, sinking into the excruciating cold of Melody Lake. She went over the well-worn path in her mind. Was there one moment, one split second of regret when her mother had reconsidered, struggling to turn toward the shore? Had she gone to her death with regret or relief?

It doesn't matter. It's done. She's gone. Uncle Paul is gone.

I'm alone.

Luca reached over and adjusted the air vents to allow the heat to blow on her, but it did not help. There was no relief. She doubted there ever would be.

"I'm not...sure what to do here," Luca said.

She blinked. "There's nothing for you to do."

"There will be details to deal with. Things that need taking care of," he returned, voice soft.

"I'll do it."

"I can help. Steph and Tate also." He shifted, his bulk seeming too big for the small front seat. "We'll interface with the police." His posture relaxed slightly, and she knew he was relieved to have constructed a plan of action. She felt suddenly angry.

"You can't fix this, Luca."

"I know that."

"Then why do you try? Why are you here now?"

"I already told you."

She wanted to shake him out of the horrible poise. "You aren't staying here for the treasure. You're doing this for my father and because you feel guilty leaving me alone now that Uncle Paul is probably dead."

He gazed out the window as if he was a tourist, taking in the sparkling view. "You need help right now, Ava. It's not a crime to admit that. I…I want to help."

The words rushed out in a furious hiss. "I don't need you."

"Your business is failing, you are dealing with the loss of a loved one and this place reminds you of your mother's suicide. You need help. Your father agrees." He turned sober green eyes on her and let out a breath. "I'm sorry. That was not kind of me to say."

He was right. She wondered why it hurt so much to have all the darkness pulled out and put on display. "If my life is such a mess," she said through clenched teeth, "then why would you want to stay here and be involved?"

"Because…" His voice trailed off and then he cleared his throat. "For whatever reason, our paths crossed and you need help. We'll stay until the treasure business is wrapped up. Then I'm gone."

Cold. Detached. All business.

How could he know what she was feeling? This man from a perfect family who never struggled with how to pay the electric bills? Who moved through the world with the confidence born of living in a stable family with loving siblings and a strong parent?

"Forget it." Ava turned away, staring out the window at the furious storm clouds marching in like soldiers across the dome of sky, the interlocking branches above sending bits of ice raining down on them.

She wiped at a fogged-over spot on the side window. The view cleared for a moment, she peered out at the world cocooned in white until the jangle of the phone disturbed the quiet.

SEVEN

He drove Ava back to Towers's location, fearing what the next few minutes would hold. Ava stood rigid, eyes fixed on one particular tree a few feet from the road. The scent of pine became almost pungent.

"They didn't say he was dead," she kept repeating. "They just said they'd found something."

"Ava, I think this is going to turn out to be bad news," he said as kindly as he could manage.

At first he thought she did not hear him, her gaze remained riveted on the pale landscape. He wished he could read her mind.

Towers appeared, walking through the swiftly falling snow. The ruined snowmobile had been located, he told them, but it was not safe to extract it until the weather cleared. The rest remained unsaid. It was not safe to continue searching for bodies, either.

Luca did not have any greater optimism that Uncle Paul had survived than he had before.

They drove back to the trailer park in silence.

"He's alive," Ava said as he eased the car into the parking place outside her trailer. "There were no bodies with the snowmobile."

Her sudden comment startled him. "I know it must seem that way."

"You still think he's dead?"

He remained quiet, trying to decide on a gentle way to give voice to his thoughts. "I'm not sure what to make of it."

"Me, neither, but until they prove me wrong, I'm going to believe he is alive."

Ava was already out and heading up the trailer steps before he unbuckled his seat belt. A car he hadn't seen before, a small white SUV, was parked nearby. Even though it was possible he was intruding, Luca followed her in anyway, exercising his "barrel right in, ask for permission later" philosophy.

A slender woman with long black hair woven into a thick braid sprang from a chair. Worry carved deep furrows into her brow and around her mouth. She enveloped Ava in a hug and pressed a kiss on her temple.

"What? Tell me," Sue Agnoti said, her hands clutching Ava's. "Did they find him?"

Ava led her back to the chair and gently pushed her into it. "Sue, this is Luca Gage, he's…helping me work with the police."

Her gaze settled on Luca for the first time it

seemed. She was probably in her mid-fifties, Luca surmised. She offered him a brilliant smile that Luca wondered if she reserved for male acquaintances.

"I'm so sorry," she said. "I heard that Paul was in an accident. The police are mum on the details except to say they haven't found him yet."

Ava explained what they'd been told.

Sue chewed her lip. After a moment, she sighed. "I knew something was going on."

Ava sat next to her and Luca settled himself on the couch that was far too low to accommodate his long legs.

"When did you see him last?" Ava demanded.

"When I cooked him poached eggs three days ago." Sue took in the surprise on their faces.

"He came by Whisper early, just after sunup. He said he wanted to see the place, to check up on things, but that was a lie, of course." Sue looked at Luca. "Oh, I don't mean to slander Paul, but he is an excellent liar. I can tell only because I've known him for so long." She smoothed her ribbed sweater across her stomach. "He wouldn't tell me what was wrong." A flash of anger lit her eyes. "I'm sorry for saying it, Ava, honey, but your uncle can be a world-class cretin."

Luca was surprised when Ava smiled. "I know, Sue. I'm sorry."

They exchanged a look that told Luca there was

plenty of history between Sue and Ava. He cleared his throat.

"What do you think Paul was really up to?"

Sue shrugged gracefully. "I wondered…" She waved a manicured hand.

"Wondered what?" Ava said.

"Well, honey, I was afraid you had really decided to sell, and he was saying his last goodbye to the place."

Ava sagged.

Sue gripped her hand. "It doesn't have to be that way. I still think we can save Whisper. I know it."

Ava looked at the hand that held hers.

"Your uncle is not a businessman, Ava. Oh, he's tried to be all that, a record producer, a car salesman, I think even a cattle baron as I recall, but the man has no head for money, charming as he is."

Ava cleared her throat. "I know."

Luca tried to find a more comfortable position on the worn couch. "Mrs. Agnoti," he began.

"Oh, please, call me Sue. Mrs. Agnoti sounds like a school principal or something."

"Sue," he returned, with a smile. "Paul might have left something at Whisper. Would it be okay if we came and took a look around the resort?"

She raised an eyebrow. "Ava can tell you, the place is in terrible condition. Harold and I try to keep it up, but there's not much two people can manage."

"Just to look," Luca said.

Sue smiled. "Can any woman say no to that face?"

He felt himself blush. "Perfect. Let's figure on tomorrow, if the storm isn't too violent and pending the search progress." He struggled free of the couch, intending to give the two women some time to chat, but Sue also rose, following him to the door.

"Storm's nearly here," she said, with a practiced eye toward the horizon. "I have just enough time to get up the mountain if I leave now." She hugged Ava. "We'll keep the faith, won't we? We'll believe that Paul is okay and we'll save this resort somehow."

Ava didn't answer.

Luca knew that deep down, she'd lost hold of that comfort. His heart squeezed. He could see the misery reflected in her soul. He also felt a flood of guilt that his father was considering buying Whisper and he hadn't said a word about it to Ava. It just didn't seem like the right time, in view of the bigger picture.

She desperately needed to believe that somehow her uncle was still alive.

Snowflakes flitted through the door as Ava saw them out and her gaze flicked toward the distant mountain ridge. Sue's did the same.

They were both thinking the same thing, he was sure.

How could a man survive another night alone on Whisper Mountain?

Luca's practical nature had the answer that no one wanted to hear.

He couldn't.

Ava was grateful that she'd packed a small duffel before her disastrous meeting with Uncle Paul. She'd intended to be away from her tiny apartment for only an afternoon, long enough to meet with Uncle Paul and contact a real estate agent, but she could not resist the lure of one more run down the pristine slopes of Whisper Mountain, so a spare set of clothes had made sense.

It was past one, and Ava hadn't managed to sleep more than a few hours before her mind drove her from bed. Hours of pacing the small kitchen, watching the grainy TV for weather reports and taking as hot a shower as the leaky faucet would allow did nothing to make the dawn come any faster. She almost wished she'd asked for Mack Dog to stay with her instead of Tate and Stephanie, but the dog had taken such a fancy to Tate that she didn't have the heart to separate them. She wondered if something about Tate reminded Mack Dog of Uncle Paul.

Thankfully, Stephanie had stocked the rattling refrigerator with some staples like orange juice, eggs and bread. She'd also left a half dozen chocolate bars on the counter. Even though Ava appreciated the gesture, she felt the twinge of resentment.

They were here for treasure. Luca had said as much.

He was after a pearl, not Uncle Paul or anyone else.

The muscles in her jaw tightened. *Go away, Luca. Find your treasure someplace else.*

Something pricked at her, a memory that did not mesh with her current view of Luca Gage. She flashed back on the image of him walking out on the ice toward her, face resolute, not a flicker of doubt. What would it be like to be sure of your choices, to know the right path and follow it with such maddening certainty?

The moment her mother died, all her certainty about everything had evaporated. She was sure of precisely nothing.

With a sigh, Ava opened a candy bar and pulled her legs underneath her, nibbling chocolate with one hand and balancing a notepad on her knee with the other. She made a neat column of notes, precise handwriting spelling out all she knew or thought she knew about her uncle's situation, so like her mother would have done. Marcia Stanton was an obsessive list maker, a trait manifested just as strongly in her daughter.

When she wrote *Taser tag,* the words kindled some hope inside her. The tiny metal circle would prove who owned the weapon. They would find out who took Uncle Paul and arrest him.

But would it be for kidnapping?

Or murder?

The chocolate turned to ash in Ava's mouth. She

put down the candy bar and the notes, wrapped herself in a blanket and decided to make a concerted effort to force herself into sleep.

Her body finally overruled her mind and she fell into an uneasy slumber. She woke, disoriented, muscles cramped as the clock ticked its way to two-thirty. The trailer was dark except for the bathroom light that she'd left on. The glow did not add any cheer to the desolate space. Uncle Paul's piles of books stood like crooked old men, a sad reminder of the person who was not there to read them.

Wind rattled against the windows, the trees outside casting eerie shadows on the glass.

She thumbed her phone to life and checked the weather. The Doppler showed the storm was indeed hammering Whisper Mountain, bringing plenty of new snow. In another season she would have celebrated the conditions that brought ski resorts to life. Before her father's accident, several unusually warm winters had provided such poor snowfall that Whisper had been forced to keep its doors closed. Another nail in the coffin for a small operation without the funds to purchase snow guns like the larger ski runs used to pad their slopes during warmer winters. She didn't feel like celebrating now.

Where are you, Uncle Paul? She closed her eyes again, determined to rest up. She would attempt another snowshoe exploration before or after their trek to Whisper Mountain.

Luca's words rang in her ears.

Bad idea.

He was right, of course, but she could think of nothing else to try.

A scuttling noise slithered near her feet.

She bolted up, heart pounding.

Something was crawling across the floor.

Heart in her throat, she snapped on the light on the table next to her. There was nothing on the ugly stained tile. She forced a deep breath. Just her over-active imagination.

Relieved, she leaned back on the sofa again and gathered the blanket around her.

The noise came again, a soft scraping moving the length of the floor. Her mind finally made sense of it. Nerves pricking she realized the sound originated not inside the trailer, but underneath it.

EIGHT

The unit, like all the others, was elevated a foot or so off the ground on raised legs which kept it level. Whatever was making the noise was crawling along slowly in the gap between the trailer floor and the ground.

Ava dismissed her initial panic. It was an animal, perhaps a rabbit or cat, seeking shelter from the storm in the relatively dry space underneath. She shot a look at Mack Dog's empty bed. Perhaps he'd gotten away from Tate and embarked on another exploration. He was a furry Houdini, her uncle maintained. She listened to the wind-driven snow pattering against the flat trailer roof.

Again her mind returned to Uncle Paul.

Please, God.

And then she stopped. Uncle Paul was a rascal who had cheated countless people. His sister, Ava's mother, was the epitome of honesty, returning fifteen miles to the store to pay for a travel magazine inadvertently stuck in her pile of groceries. Marcia was dead. The irony was impossible to miss. A woman who attended church faithfully and prayed unceasingly was snatched away. God had not saved her from the crushing depression that worsened after Bruce was crippled and the resort slipped further out of their hands. Ava's crude prayer for a man who was most definitely a sinner was a waste of time. God wasn't in the saving business, good or bad.

She squeezed her eyes shut tight and tried to blot out the sound of the storm. The slithering from underneath the trailer came again, louder this time. Ava got up and threw off the blanket. The noise was too loud for a rabbit or raccoon. Dollars to doughnuts it was Mack Dog. Ava had never been much of a dog person, preferring the reserved aloofness of cats. Mack Dog was certainly not the smartest critter, but Uncle Paul loved him, mauled snowshoes notwithstanding.

She pulled on a jacket and boots.

"You'd better come when I call you, dog," she grumbled, snatching a flashlight from a tiny kitchen drawer.

A blast of super-cooled air hit her like a fist as she stepped carefully through the snow that had accumulated on the porch step. A light fixed on a pole near the office trailer backlit the lacy curtain of flakes that danced down from the blackened sky. The campground was perfectly quiet.

She tottered down the steps and into a shin-deep

pile of snow at the bottom. The cold seeped through the thin material of her sweats and made her gasp. She headed for the spot where the wheel was sandwiched between two wooden wedges and beamed her flashlight into the gap underneath, expecting to see the eerie glow of animal eyes peering back at her before whatever it was made a quick retreat.

Only one animal would answer her call and come to the crazy woman clomping around in the snow before sunup.

"Mack Dog?" she whispered. "If that's you, come out of there right now."

There was no sound and she could not see anything in the darkened space. Could be the trespasser had taken off, but she had to give it one more try if her conscience was going to allow her some rest before sunup.

"Treat, Mack Dog," she called, scooting closer to the gap. She bent near to repeat the hopeful suggestion when something grabbed her ankles. She went over on her back, the wind knocked out of her, as she fell into a blanket of snow.

She tried to turn over on her stomach, but the snowy shroud offered no place to grab. She screamed, but the sound seemed to be absorbed, snow falling into her open mouth and blinding her.

The sky shifted and moved before her very eyes.

She was being slowly dragged into the blackness beneath the trailer.

* * *

Luca could not sleep. His legs itched to go for a run. Surely he could find a snowplowed road somewhere. A good run with nothing but the moon and his own thoughts for company. Maybe it was just what he needed to understand how he had managed to wind up with two feet firmly planted in Ava's world. The truth was, he had nursed a crush on Ava when he was a teen. What red-blooded boy wouldn't look on that blend of delicate beauty and ferocious athleticism without having his head turned? But he wasn't a boy any longer, so why did he find her occupying his every thought?

One look out at the swirling storm put the lid on his notion to go for a run. He settled instead on doing sit-ups and pull-ups until he'd fended off the chill in his dingy trailer and restored his mind to some resemblance of calm. It didn't work completely. Knowing that Ava was a hundred feet away, planning to go search for her uncle again at first light made his nerves jangle. Something drew him to the window and he looked across at her trailer. The falling snow accumulated in airy drifts on her porch steps and everything was still and quiet.

Except for the sudden extinguishing of a small light, as if it had been flung suddenly down in the snow. Muscles tensed, he threw a pair of boots over his sweatpants and ran into the night, pulling on a shirt as he galloped to her trailer. Now that he was closer, he heard muffled gasps, the sound of hands scrabbling for purchase on the snow. He beelined toward the sound.

At first he could not make out what was happening in the dim light. Something was flailing around, but he could not tell who or what it was. He plunged a hand toward the writhing lump and grabbed what felt like a handful of jacket.

Incredibly, he saw Ava's head rise slightly above the level of the snow, her eyes wide, gasping for breath. She opened her mouth to speak, but he watched in amazement as she was yanked from his grasp, hauled to her knees underneath the trailer.

He didn't stop to puzzle it out.

He grabbed hold of her shoulders and pulled as hard as he had done at the last Gage family tug-of-war. Her body slid loose and they both tumbled backward. Breath whooshed out of both of them as they wound up sprawled in the snow. He immediately shot to his feet, hauled her upright.

Something scraped and wriggled frantically, heading for the rear of the trailer. He raced around the corner, just in time to see someone emerge from under the trailer and take off toward the tree line.

"Stop!" he shouted. Even though his tone was thunderous, it hardly carried over the wind. Luca ran faster. He would overtake the guy, no doubt about it, the gap between them was already closing. Head down he sprinted faster, hand outstretched as he came closer, the dark jacket and knit cap now clear in the moonlight.

When he was within inches, the runner suddenly reversed course, zigzagging wide around Luca, leaving him to turn and regain his balance. Now the pursuit changed in the direction of the office trailer. Whoever it was must have a car parked at the entrance or farther beyond, somewhere along the main road.

Luca dug down and moved as fast as his legs would allow. The snow between the trailers was still not very deep due to the plowing it had received the day before. He was able to once again close the distance between them. This time, there was no escaping.

The figure rounded the corner of the trailer and Luca did the same.

Gotcha, he thought.

The momentary celebration was driven from his mind as a wooden bat appeared before him, smashing into his solar plexus before he could alter course.

He went down, face-first, pain lancing through him.

Even in his prone position he tried to get his knees under him, knowing the bat was probably descending to crush his skull. Instead a rough hand reached out and flipped him over. Blinded by the snow, he threw up an arm to ward off the blow he knew was coming.

"No, don't," a voice said.

In spite of the gasping of his own breath, he heard Ava repeat it again. "Don't hit him."

Luca shook the snow from his eyes and found himself looking into the face of Bully, arms still hoisting a bat overhead.

Bully's eyes cut from Ava to Luca as he slowly lowered the bat. "What ya running around like that for? I thought you was a rapist or something."

Luca was still struggling to suck in a breath, so Ava filled him in. "Did you see the other person? The one Luca was chasing?"

"Nah." Bully scanned the snowy landscape. "Whoever it was is long gone. I was just on my way to get a drink of orange juice and I seen someone running, so I got my bat. Sorry about that, chum." Bully offered Luca his palm.

Upright, Luca found himself hunched over, trying to breathe through the pain in his stomach.

Ava put a tentative hand on his arm. "Are you okay?"

Luca managed a nod. "Reminds me of high school football days," he gasped. *Only worse.*

"Come on in before we all freeze to death," Bully said, slamming open the door to his trailer.

Ava took Luca's arm and led him up the steps.

"Make yourself at home," Bully called out, heading for the kitchen. "I'll nuke some coffee."

Luca sank down on the couch, finally able to focus on Ava. "What about you? Are you bleeding?"

She dabbed at her mouth with her jacket sleeve. "Just cut my lip when whoever that was took the legs from under me." She sat dejectedly on an ottoman, upholstered with the Laker's basketball team logo. "I thought it was Mack Dog. Dumb."

Luca felt a stab of pity for her. "Not dumb. Wouldn't expect someone to be hunkered down under your trailer."

Bully returned with cups of hot instant coffee. "What was he doin' under your trailer?"

Ava sipped the coffee. "I can't imagine. For a moment, I thought…"

Luca didn't press. He knew what she'd thought.

Bully slurped into his cup. "Thought what?"

"That my uncle had come back."

Bully started. "I figured he was…well…you know."

"They haven't found a body," Ava said, chin high. "He could be alive."

"Hmm." Bully cocked his head, which seemed only to widen his cheeks even more. "He's a cagey one. Wouldn't put it past him to be holed up somewhere. I seen him do some strange things."

"Like what?" Ava pressed.

Rolling the mug between his calloused palms, Bully considered. "Now I think on it, he was crawling around under that trailer a time or two."

Luca was finally able to draw a full breath. "When?"

"Last week. I asked him what he was doin' under

there. Said he was discouraging a family of cats from setting up residence." Bully slowly shook his head. "I ain't noticed a family of cats around here recently. Especially not with Mack Dog staying on the property."

Luca's eyes locked on Ava's. He could see the thoughts twirling madly in her mind.

"Maybe Uncle Paul hid something there, and he came back for it."

Luca shook his head. "Then why did he run? Why would he pull you under the trailer in the first place?"

She did not lose the stubborn set to her chin. "He didn't know it was me."

Luca frowned. She was grasping at straws. "It seems more likely that someone else came here to search under the trailer. Someone who knew that Paul had something valuable in his possession."

Bully snorted. "Paul was always more talk than walk. Some fake cameos and gold-plated junk is probably all he had."

"Not this time," Ava said. "This time he had something worth abducting him for."

The big man grimaced. "Now you know he was my friend, honey, but that don't mean I can't see the truth about him. Plenty of people would like a shot at getting even with old Pauly, treasure or no."

"What about you?" Ava shot back. "Did you have any reason to get back at my uncle?"

Bully frowned. "You're upset. I guess that gives

you the right to say things like that, but I been nothing but good to your uncle even when he skipped out without paying. I still let him stay here, though, didn't I? I been nicer to him than anyone else in town."

Ava shoulders drooped. "I'm sorry, Bully. You've been a good friend. I'll pay you what he owes in back rent."

Bully patted her shoulder. "Don't mind about that. You got your hands full. I just want you to know I'm on your side in all this."

Ava got up and moved to the door. "I'm going to look under the trailer."

"Wait until morning," Luca said. "You won't see much in the dark with this storm."

"That's what flashlights are for," Ava shot over her shoulder as she disappeared into the night.

Bully raised a thick eyebrow. "She ain't big on the waiting-around thing?"

"No," Luca snapped. *She's not big on the being-reasonable thing, either.*

Bully clapped him on the back, a move that sent painful reverberations along his rib cage. "Guess you better go catch up, then, sport."

Luca bit back a remark as he headed into the night after her.

NINE

Ava made it back to the trailer quickly in spite of the blowing snow. She stopped long enough inside to grab a better flashlight. Luca made it just as she shone her light into the gap under the trailer, his hand held to his stomach.

"You should go back to bed. You don't look so good."

His lip curled. "You try taking a grand slam to the solar plexus."

She hid a smile at the look on his face and prepared to shimmy back under in the same spot she'd been dragged only a short time before. Luca crouched next to her, eyeing the gap.

"I know what you're thinking, and you're too big."

Luca huffed. "I can make it."

"Okay," Avery said, slithering into the dark space, "but don't blame me if we have to use a crowbar to get you out."

She didn't catch his disgruntled comment as the

darkness closed around her. It was tight quarters, the bottom of the trailer seemed to press down on her shoulders. Even though the space was clear of snow, it smelled of mold, which no doubt clung to the wooden braces that shored up the floor and helped level out the contraption. She shined her flashlight into the darkness.

Another beam of light crossed hers as Luca dropped to his stomach and aimed the flashlight she'd discarded in her direction.

"Hey," she said, throwing a hand over her eyes.

"Sorry." Luca repositioned the light. "That's probably what happened to the guy under the trailer. You momentarily blinded him."

"Maybe." She continued her search, avoiding a pile of droppings left by a raccoon or rabbit. "But who was it and what was he doing under here in the first place?"

"That's the million-dollar question." Luca's light caught something nestled in the farthest corner of the trailer. "What's that?"

Ava wriggled deeper toward the far corner, her excitement edging up a notch as she closed in. "Oh man."

"What? What is it?" Luca practically yelled.

"Just a minute." Ava reached out a hand to the wooden box. Someone had laid it carefully on a series of bricks. To raise it off the damp ground? It was long, maybe twenty-six inches wide and shallow, not quite ten inches tall. She pulled at it, but her awkward angle and the unruly size of the box made it difficult.

In the meantime, Luca was pushing farther into the space, as far as his wide shoulders would allow. "What's in it?"

"I don't know. There's not enough clearance here to open it. I'll have to drag it out." She lugged the box inch by inch toward her makeshift entrance. When she was within arm's reach, Luca took hold of it and slid it out, returning immediately to hold Avery's flashlight. When she struggled free, he helped her to her feet.

"Come on," Ava said, hurrying back up the porch steps. She felt a new urgency, hope swirling around inside her that whatever the mystery box contained might be the clue to finding her uncle.

Luca thumped up the steps beside her and they turned on the lights, blinking as their eyes adjusted. He carried the box to the table and set it down. She could see he was itching to open it, fingers curled in anticipation.

He nodded to her. "You do the honors."

Pleased, somehow, at the small chivalry, she unhooked the metal latch on the box and slowly opened the lid.

They stood shoulder to shoulder peering into an empty box.

Ava could not contain her sigh as she sank down into a chair. "Nothing. Nothing at all." She blinked hard as the night caught up with her. She would not cry. Tears were useless anyway.

Luca frowned into the interior. "One thing you learn in the treasure seeking business is how to mine all the clues you can from every find."

Ava straightened. "There are clues here?"

He opened the box completely so the hinged lid rested on the table. "For one thing, someone fixed a metal liner in the bottom. It's a homemade job, so there's the possibility there are fingerprints, but the bigger issue seems to me to be what was in the box?"

"Something pretty valuable," Ava breathed. "For someone to go to the trouble of making a box and hiding it under the trailer."

Luca considered. "Seems silly, though. Why not put it in a safe-deposit box? Completely anonymous and ultra-secure."

Ava laughed. "Well, if this is Uncle Paul's handiwork, I can tell you he doesn't trust banks. Or cops. Or the government. Or pretty much anyone. He says they're all scammers and he should know."

Luca chuckled, bending closer to the box. "Do you have a magnifying glass?"

"Yes, I found one in the kitchen drawer." She got it and moved close until her shoulder brushed his muscled arm. The faint scent of soap clung to him and she enjoyed the musky fragrance. "What do you see?"

He used the magnifying glass to peer closely at

the miniscule gap between the wooden box and its metal liner. The space was no bigger than pinky width. Luca abruptly grabbed a knife from the block on the counter. He inserted the tip gingerly into the sliver of space. When he pulled it clear again, an earring dangled from the point.

They both stared at the single drop pearl, an iridescent, milky white.

"I wonder," Ava said, her voice barely a whisper, "where Uncle Paul got that."

Luca asked for a plastic bag and laid the earring carefully on top while he photographed it. Then he slid it inside and closed the top. His face was alight with discovery, and he exuded an energy that Ava found was catching.

"Do you think it's the treasure you're after?"

"Not likely. The Sunset Star is a pink pearl and it's set into a pendant, or it was anyway, the last time it was photographed."

He was moving on now, studying the outside of the box. Ava did the same on the side closest to her.

Her heart leaped. "Look!" She could barely make out some pencil scratches on the side of the box. She grabbed the magnifying glass and squinted at it. "Letters? No, numbers." She rattled them off to Luca.

"Seven digits. A telephone number minus the area code, so it's for someplace local."

"I'll get a pencil." Nerves jangling with excitement, she went for the notepad nearest the phone.

Her hand was arrested in mid-motion as she reached for the pencil.

Luca gave her a questioning look.

"I don't have to write it down," she said slowly. "It's already here on this notepad, right next to a name."

"Whose?"

"Charlie Goren, the friend of my uncle who called earlier."

Luca wasn't sure what to make of the phone number. Neither was Ava apparently, because she began to pace the cramped space, eyes darting in thought.

"I'm trying to remember the name, if Uncle Paul ever talked about Goren."

He took out his smartphone and plugged the name and number into an internet search. He didn't have to wait long. "Charlie Goren owns an antique jewelry store in Lofton."

She stared at him. "That's an hour from here."

"It sure is." He checked the time. "Unfortunately, it's only a little after four-thirty. His store doesn't open until eight."

Her eyes were wide, lips parted. His heart sped up as she spoke.

"If we get there right when it opens, we can talk to him and be back at the search site before ten."

He knew she had every intention of going out again to search for her uncle the moment the storm passed, regardless of what the police said. For some reason he could not fathom, he would, of course, be going along with her.

"We could call Goren," Luca suggested.

"I'd rather talk to him face to face."

"You think he might be involved with your uncle's accident?"

Ava shrugged. "I don't know, but I just feel like I need to eyeball him myself and I don't want to pull any cops away from the search." Ava marched to the kitchen and began gathering things from the fridge.

He watched her precise movements, admiring her natural grace, wishing he could reach out and touch that shimmering bob of hair. What was the matter with him?

"I'll call the police," Luca said. "Fill them in on the box and the phone number and get Stephanie and Tate over here to check things out before the police confiscate everything."

"Okay. I'm making us some breakfast. I'll make enough for four."

He raised an eyebrow. He hadn't expected her to offer to cook for them. Even though he normally put himself in charge of culinary affairs, he knew it was important to her to keep busy. "That will be great."

"Well, all I know how to fix is scrambled eggs and toast, so it might not be exactly great, but it will fill us up and pass the time until we go see Goren."

He couldn't argue with that logic. He left a message for the sergeant and texted his sister.

She and Tate arrived along with Mack Dog in fifteen minutes.

Tate looked wide-awake as he helped himself to scrambled eggs and coffee. He offered a quiet greeting

Stephanie had the aura of someone rousted out of bed far too early. She glared at her brother. "I imagine this could not have waited another three hours?"

He grinned and showed her the earring. The fatigue slipped from her face as she snatched the bag from his hands. "Obviously it's not the Sunset Star, but it might be part of Danson's collection. That would be a clear indication that we're on the right track." She rolled the pearl gently between her fingers.

"Is it real?" Luca said around a mouthful of egg.

"Hard to say. I'd put it between my teeth, but I doubt the cops would appreciate my contaminating the evidence."

"You that hungry?" Tate teased.

She gave him a wry smile. "No, smarty pants. If the surface is gritty, it's a natural or cultured pearl, not fake. You can also take an X-ray. If you see layers like an onion skin, it's a natural pearl." She shot a look at her brother. "I could have it authenticated back in San Francisco. Are you sure we need to…"

"Yes," both Tate and Luca said at once.

Her cheeks pinked. "All right, all right. I know we have to hand it over to the police. I was just thinking about delaying a bit."

"No way. By the book," Luca said.

"You sound like Victor."

"Our big brother makes sense on rare occasions." Luca drained his coffee. "So who's doing what today?"

Tate offered to head to the search site. "I can take Mack Dog with me and deliver the box to the police. I'll keep everyone posted."

Ava nodded gratefully. "Thank you. I'll be back as soon as I talk to Goren."

"We'll be back," Luca corrected.

Ava looked away, brows drawn. "I don't need a chaperone."

"True, but you don't know anything about pearls do you?"

"Neither do you," she shot back.

"But I do," Stephanie said. "So I'll invite myself along and keep the two of you on your best behavior."

Luca and Ava both stared at Stephanie. She laughed. "We're hunting for treasure, aren't we? The more eyes the better."

Luca noticed that Ava did not meet his gaze as she finished her breakfast. She still thought she could find her uncle and figure out what happened all by her lonesome. He wondered why that both exasperated and pleased him.

He dismissed the thought as they each went about their preparations for departure. He helped clear the dishes and dry after Ava washed. They didn't speak. That was probably better anyway.

He was putting away the last dish when the trailer phone rang.

There was no answer to his "Hello," but someone stayed on the line.

"Who is this? Who are you trying to reach?"

Click.

A tickle of worry rippled through his stomach.

It was the same anonymous caller as before, he was sure of it.

Ava shrugged it off. "Some prankster? It doesn't matter. I just know Goren will be able to help us figure out what happened to my uncle."

He heard it in her voice. The unspoken statement.

So I can bring him home.

Ava, he thought, *I really hope you're right.*

All the same, he made a mental note to let the police know about the calls.

The time ticked by slowly. Tate had already gone to the search site when Stephanie, Luca and Ava piled into the car and began the painfully slow drive down the mountain. Snow was still falling, but the worst of the wind had passed, leaving the landscape a perfect crystalline world. They marveled in silence as Ava guided the car along the road crowded by trees sparkling in the watery sunrise.

Beautiful, he thought, gazing past Ava's perfect delicate profile at the wondrous landscape beyond.

They had to creep along until they made it to a plowed road which allowed them to reach Lofton in a little under an hour. Ava was out of the car and almost to the door of the small shop by the time they caught up.

She yanked on the handle, her face falling when she found it locked, knocking on the glass anyway.

Stephanie checked her phone. "It's eight-fifteen. Maybe they run on their own timetable around here."

They peered into the darkened shop. Luca could make out encased glassed shelves and a main counter.

"Let's go around the back," he whispered.

While Stephanie stayed in the front to call the store phone, Luca and Ava headed toward the rear, pushing across drifts of snow that piled the walkway. There was only one window and it was shuttered.

The metal door was closed, too, but Luca knocked anyway.

Nothing moved inside the shop, nothing that they could see anyway.

Ava bit her lip. "I need to talk to him, but I want to get back to the search."

"We can split up."

Ava opened her mouth to answer, when a shadow

loomed up behind her. He tensed in shock as a man appeared around the edge of the store with a shotgun and pressed it to the back of Ava's head.

TEN

Ava did not feel fear at first. She was too surprised. The circle of metal against her skull did not compute, but the look of rage on Luca's face did.

He shot a hand toward the gunman. "She's not doing anything wrong. Back off."

The pressure did not wane. The assailant was not close enough for her to kick out, she didn't think. She could not come up with a plan due to the blood that seemed to rush wildly through her body and rob her of her senses.

Luca edged closer. "Lower the gun," he growled at whoever was behind her.

"What do you want?" came a man's voice, higher than she might have expected, with a slight wobble.

"We came to talk to Charlie Goren. Is that you?" Ava said, surprised that her own words came out clear and strong in spite of the tremor that had spread throughout her body.

"Who wants to know?" The man pressed the gun harder, and Ava winced. Luca's face reddened.

"Get off her now." He took another step forward just as Stephanie rounded the corner.

Luca used the moment of distraction to surge forward and strike the gun away from Ava's head. He shoved her aside and kicked out at the gunman, sending him falling onto his back in the snow.

Ava and Stephanie both stared open-mouthed.

"I'm gone two minutes, and you run into a gunman?" Stephanie said.

Luca picked up the gun and stood like an angry bear over the prostrate man. "Get up," he ordered, flicking a glance at Ava. "Are you all right?"

She nodded, still in shock.

The man slowly got to his feet, hand clamped to his stomach where Luca had kicked him. He was small, with dark hair and dark eyes, Asian or at least partially of Asian descent, Ava surmised now that she had recovered slightly from having a gun pressed to her head.

"You're trespassing," the man said, black eyes shifting from Luca to Ava and Stephanie.

Ava eased closer in spite of Luca's warning glare. "Are you Charlie Goren?"

After a momentary pause, he nodded. "This is my store," he said, an edge of pride in his tone. "I have the right to protect it, especially after everything that's happened."

"Yeah?" Luca said, examining the gun. "Well, you're not much of a security guard. You know the shotgun isn't even loaded?"

"I know," Goren said. "I figured it would be just as frightening loaded as empty."

He was right about that, Ava thought. "I'm Paul's niece."

Goren started at the name. "You are?"

She nodded. "Do you know my uncle?"

"Sure. I've known Paul since we washed dishes together in a diner when we were in our twenties. I heard he was in some trouble."

"You left a message on my cell phone that you wanted to talk to me."

He nodded. "Have they—" he swallowed hard "—found him?"

Ava resisted a shudder. "No, but I think he's still alive." Luca shot her a warning look, but she ignored him.

Stephanie edged closer. "Look, because we've established there's no need for a shooting, can we go inside, Mr. Goren? I'm freezing, and we obviously have a few things to discuss."

Goren seemed to snap out of his stupor. He unlocked the door and led them inside. The shop smelled of old wood. Faded velvet backdrops offered up various antique pendants, rings and necklaces.

"Did my uncle contact you recently?"

"Yes, about a week ago he showed up. I hadn't seen him for a couple of years at least." Goren's eyes narrowed. "He needed money from me, and I loaned it to him, which makes me a dope, I guess."

Money which he obviously hadn't paid back. Ava gulped. Was there anyone Paul hadn't crossed? "Did he say why he needed the money?"

"He was going to bid on an abandoned storage unit. If there was anything of value inside, we'd split the profit. Said he'd been doing some research and he figured the unit belonged to a man named…" Goren squinted. "I can't remember, but he was an eccentric from a wealthy family."

"John Danson?" Luca offered.

"Yes, Danson. That's right. Paul bid on the unit and bought the contents."

Ava's heart sped up. "Did you find out what was inside?"

A look of disgust crept onto Goren's face. "Some old books, odds and ends. Some jewelry. Cheap, hardly enough to make us wealthy or enough even to recoup our investment. Not the big payoff Paul convinced me we'd find."

Luca showed him the picture of the earring. "Was this one of the pieces you saw?"

Goren peered closely, then straightened. "No, no, it wasn't. Where did you get it?"

"My uncle's trailer," Ava said.

Goren shook his head, and rubbed a hand through his dark hair seeded with silver. "I would be surprised if Paul didn't lie about what was in that box. He probably showed me some worthless pieces and kept the good ones for himself. Said he didn't have enough to pay me back the money I loaned him."

Ava looked around the dingy shop. She felt ashamed that her uncle had cheated this man of humble means. "I'm sorry."

"Me, too. Paul talked about the pearl, a fantastic pearl." Goren's eyes lit up. "I let my own desire get the best of my judgment." He spread his hands. "I'm passionate about gems."

Stephanie peered into a case containing an antique brooch with a green stone. "You've got some nice pieces."

"Yes," he said, straightening. "That one right there is an emerald of the finest water."

"Water?" Luca said.

Stephanie nodded. "It's old language. With emeralds the clarity or crystal is just as important as the color. Jewelers refer to it as the water of the stone."

Goren was beaming now. "My customers usually don't know anything about gems. I have to educate them." He beckoned to Stephanie. "Come see this piece. It's small but extremely fine. You can see the star pattern clearly…"

Stephanie offered a charming smile. "I would love to, but we're kind of in a time crunch, Mr. Goren. Could you tell us why you were trying to reach Ava?"

Goren's smile dimmed. He looked away, snatching up a cloth to buff the glass countertop. "I'm ashamed to admit it, but—" he glanced quickly at Ava and then away again "—I heard Paul was missing and I figured maybe he'd left the rest of the storage unit contents behind." He sighed. "I didn't want anything to happen to your uncle, but I figured if I could get the jewelry, even though it wasn't great stuff, maybe I could make back some of the money I loaned him."

Ava watched him rub at the already-pristine counter. "We didn't find anything yet."

He finally looked up. "I'm sorry. I know it makes me sound like a heel, but I just wanted to recoup some of my money. Maybe I wouldn't feel like such a fool then."

Ava felt tears prick her eyes. She thought about how many times she'd trusted her uncle's great ideas, the occasions her mother went to bat for Paul against her own husband, the way he'd treated Sue Agnoti. "I understand, Mr. Goren, and if we find anything, we'll let you know."

They said goodbye and walked back to the car. Ava could not shake the cold feeling in the pit of her stomach. Luca and Stephanie were silent. She guessed they, too, were thinking about Uncle Paul and his habit of using and discarding those around him.

Luca broke the spell first. "Paul didn't tell Goren about the nicer pieces he found in the box. That means he could very well have found the Sunset Star and hidden it before he went to meet you. He could have been keeping it in the box under the trailer and someone tried to steal it, so he moved it to a second location. The question is, where?"

Ava brushed the sprinkle of snow from her face. The sky had cleared somewhat, revealing patches of startling azure between puffs of white clouds. "No," she said firmly. "The question in my mind is, where is Uncle Paul?" She got into the car. "I need to get back to the crash site and do some looking around on my own."

As they drove away from town, her gaze wandered to the distant peaks, to Whisper Mountain, the place where her heart always returned in spite of herself, the place where she and Luca had spent joyful winters wrapped in the innocence of youth.

If Paul had hidden a fabulous treasure, that's where he would have done it, she knew, but for now, the treasure would have to wait.

Luca once again loaded his snowshoes next to Ava's before they drove up to the search site. Ava sat perfectly erect, taking in every detail of the glittering landscape as they approached. There had been no additional contact with the police after they'd found the wrecked snowmobile, no word about the Taser tags and no further anonymous phone calls. If no news was good news, why did he feel so on edge?

Maybe her prayers had been answered and Paul had survived. He realized with a start that he had not once prayed for Uncle Paul directly, only for Ava. The fact of the matter was he did not like Uncle Paul, the schemer, the manipulator, a man who took advantage of so many, particularly the graceful woman who sat beside him. Ava would love him to the grave in spite of his flaws. She was the kind of person who gave her heart fully and completely to those lucky enough to be loved by her.

Luca felt another stab of guilt. Wouldn't he do the very same thing for his own family? And she had so precious little family left. Underneath her dogged belief that Paul was still alive was the naked fear of how she would deal with his loss.

Even though he could not fully understand it, he knew that some of that fear was entwined with her mother's suicide all those years before. He'd lost his own mother at such a young age that he could hardly remember her. Which was worse? he wondered. No memories at all or the memories that could drown you?

This time, he murmured a prayer for Uncle Paul.

"Let's start our search farther west," Ava was saying. "He got away from his kidnapper somehow and probably headed for the road, maybe sticking to the shoulder where the snow was not as deep. He would have made shelter from the storm along the road somewhere."

Luca eased the car around a corner, he saw a police car parked in the snow, another officer holding a rope and peering over the side.

Sergeant Towers spoke into a radio. A four-wheel-drive vehicle sat empty behind the sergeant's.

Ava hopped out and trotted over to Towers.

"Have you found anything?"

Towers appeared distracted. He held up a finger to quiet her and turned away to finish the radio conversation.

Luca caught only three words.

Bringing him up.

"Ava…" he started.

"Did you hear that?" Her face was alive with joy. "They found him. They're bringing him up."

She grabbed Luca's hand and squeezed, so close he could feel the energy vibrating through her. *God, help me know how to do this.*

He pulled her close, tucking her head under his chin. "Honey, this isn't what you think it is." It was clear from Towers's face, from the fact that there were no frantic calls for ambulance or paramedics, no hurried urgency on the part of the rescuers.

What could he do to shield her from the anguish that would cut her heart in two in a matter of moments? He wished he could take the grief for her, divert it away from her tender soul. In a state of agony, he could only clasp her to his chest and hold in the last few precious moments of hope before it melted away like a snowflake. She tried to pull away, but he held her as the stretcher cleared the top of the slope, sliding on a network of rescue ropes.

"Luca, let me go," she said, squirming hard enough to bring herself to arm's length. He still held tight to her wrists as if by anchoring her to him he could keep her from the pain that lay just behind her.

"Ava, you need to listen to me now," he said quietly.

"No." The first flicker of fear licked at her eyes. "I want to see my uncle. Let go." She tugged hard.

"Your uncle…" He did not want to say it, but his silence made the fear flame higher.

"I want to see him," she said, jerking wildly now. "I want to see him," she yelled.

Towers joined them. "Miss Stanton, I'm very sorry."

She stopped jerking and looked at him. "Don't say that. Don't say you're sorry. I don't ever want to hear that again. Not from you."

Towers regarded her quietly. "He's dead, Miss Stanton."

She yanked so hard then that she pulled from Luca's grip, tumbling backward into the snow.

Luca reached for her, but she scrambled back, face white except for the patches of color on each cheek.

"Don't touch me," she whispered. "Don't anyone touch me."

He stood frozen, his heart feeling like it had somehow fractured, too.

Slowly she got to her feet and walked to the stretcher that held the last of her hopes. Towers nodded at the officer to step away from the stretcher and he did so, standing respectfully back as Ava knelt in the snow.

"She said the same thing then," Towers said.

"What?" Luca managed.

"I was the officer who told her about her mother after they pulled her body from the lake. 'Don't touch me.' That's what she said then, too."

Luca closed his eyes and listened to the sound of Ava's sobbing, the mountains throwing her grief back in mocking echoes.

ELEVEN

Sometime later Ava found herself back in her trailer. She had only a vague recollection of Luca pulling her up out of the snow and carrying her to the car. When they arrived back at Peak Season, Stephanie stripped off Ava's wet jeans and bundled her into a robe and warm socks, forcing a mug of tea into her hands.

"I'm fine, please leave me alone," she remembered saying.

And now she was.

Alone.

The old clock above the door ticked away the seconds, the minutes.

She could not think. She could not feel.

The phone rang. She answered with a hello, normal, routine, as if it was any other day, as if she hadn't just kissed her uncle's cold cheek before the coroner took his body away.

"Avy," her father said, "Luca called me. I'm on my way just as soon as this infection clears."

Something hard and angry rose inside her. "No," she said, her voice oddly flat. "I don't want you to come."

A pause. "I know you're upset. I want to help. I love you."

"I know that, but you didn't love Uncle Paul." She swallowed against the thickening in her throat. "You despised him."

He sighed. "But you loved him, and I know you're hurting."

"I don't want you here, pretending you're sad." The tears fell now, coursing down her face and soaking into the threads of the robe. "There's a pack of people in this town who wanted Paul dead, and now he is. I'm sure they will be celebrating." Her tone was strident, grating in her own ears.

"Stop that, Ava."

"Mom wanted you to love Paul and you didn't. You hated him."

"Not true."

"Yes, it is. All those fights. 'He's stealing you blind,' you'd say to Mom, but all she wanted was to take care of her brother. You should have tried to love him." She was sobbing now. "Mom wanted you to love him and so did I and now it's too late."

"Ava," her father said, voice broken. "Your mother and I loved each other, that's what mattered."

"So why did she kill herself, then, Dad?" Ava cried. "Answer me that? If she loved you and me so much, then why did she drown herself in that lake?" The words burned her throat like acid, but she could not stop. "Mom left us on purpose. She turned her back on you and me and God and left us."

"We don't know what happened in those final moments. She was sick. She struggled with depression all her life. You know that."

His voice seemed to come from very far away.

"She was weak and she left me. She left me." The phone was slick in her tear-wetted hand. "Uncle Paul left me, too, but at least he didn't do it on purpose."

"I will come when I can, Avy, and we'll talk this out."

"No," she sobbed. "I don't want anyone with me. Leave me alone." She slammed the phone down. It rang several more times, but she did not answer.

Her heart was iced over and only a dull throbbing ache penetrated the chill.

People passed by outside the trailer. She heard Bully, demanding answers from Luca and Stephanie who conversed with Sergeant Towers. She dimly remembered talking to him after they took her uncle away.

There would be an autopsy.

She would be notified when the body would be released.

Then there would be a funeral, she supposed. But who would come? Besides herself, who would care that Uncle Paul was dead? Killed by whoever dragged him out of her hands?

There was a knock on the door. She didn't move. Another knock, then Luca stuck his head in.

"May I come in?"

She nodded, even though she did not want to see Luca, another person who probably thought the world was better off without her uncle in it.

He stood hesitantly by the kitchen table, hands in his pockets. "Just wanted to see if you needed anything."

"Nothing, thanks."

His eyes roved the trailer, scanning everything but avoiding her face. "I'm not too good at saying the right thing. Seems dumb to ask how you are in view of what you've just experienced." He cleared his throat. "I just want you to know that we're going to help in any way we can."

"To find Paul's treasure?" she said quietly.

He blinked. "Yes."

She regarded him silently. "Because you're a treasure hunter?"

Luca moved closer and sat on a chair. "Because the treasure will show us the truth."

"About what happened to him."

Luca nodded. "Ava, I know how much he meant to you, and I'm really sorry. I'm praying for you. I want to help somehow."

She rose and turned her back on him. "Don't pray for me, Luca. It's a waste of breath."

He moved to her then, put his hand on her shoulder, gently, as if she might break. His fingers stroked her shoulders tenderly. "When Victor lost his first wife, we were there in the hospital praying with all our strength for her to pull through."

Ava turned around and found herself in the circle of his arms. "But she died."

"Yes, she did." His eyes played over her face, the warmth of his hands the only thing she could feel.

"Even though you prayed, begged, entreated on your knees, God let her die." Her voice broke as she said the words.

"Yes."

"Then how can you still pray, Luca?" She felt suddenly desperate to decipher what she saw shimmering in his green eyes.

He was silent for a moment. "Because He never promised a pain-free life for any of us here. It's just a stopping point along the way to somewhere better. I believe He knows how hard that is for us sometimes."

Deep grief and fear circled through her. She pushed her face to his, pressing her cheek hard against his chin. He responded by tightening his grip. Suddenly she wanted to lose herself in that embrace, to stay there and let Luca Gage drive away the dark shadows that crowded in all around her. "I feel like I'm drowning. I can't pray. I can't pray anymore."

He clasped her close. "Then I'll pray for both of us."

She stayed there, listening to his breathing, slow and steady, the soft murmur of his words. Her heart slowed until it matched his, beating sure and steady. Her body responded to his, melting into his arms in a flood of sweet emotion until the pain overflowed the comfort. Luca was here for the pearl. Not for anything else. She broke away.

"All right. We've got to find this treasure my uncle was hiding," she said, wiping her eyes.

He gave her a questioning look. "Are you sure you're up to this, Ava?"

"It's the only way to find out what happened. If he hid something, he would have left it at Whisper. I'll call Sue Agnoti and let her know we're coming. She'll want to know…" Ava swallowed. "I'll tell her about Paul, too," she said softly.

Luca still looked uncertain. "If your uncle hid something on Whisper Mountain, then chances are somebody else knows about it."

She resisted a shiver. "Do you think that's who was looking under the trailer last night? Maybe even the same person who abducted him?"

"I don't know, but I think until this thing is over we should be cautious."

He said goodbye and left, reluctantly, she thought. She watched out the window as he marched, shoulders hunched in thought, to his trailer. Would there ever be a time when she would not mourn the loss of her irascible uncle? Or the ache of her mother's tragic decision?

It was as if she could still feel the warmth of Luca's skin against her cheek.

It's just a stopping point along the way to somewhere better.

She wondered why the feel of his arms around her lingered in her heart, lifting one tiny corner of the smothering curtain of grief.

As the afternoon crept on toward evening, the details were settled. Sue insisted that Ava, Luca, Stephanie, Tate and the ever-present Mack Dog, come and stay at the lodge. She and her husband would see to the details.

Luca got into the driver's seat of Ava's car, worried when she didn't fuss about it. She was quiet, eyes deeply shadowed, lips tightly shut. He wished she would talk, snap at him, something. Instead, she remained silent as they headed up the mountain toward the defunct resort.

Stephanie and Tate followed behind. The road was plowed until they turned off the main stretch and began the steep ascent toward Whisper Lodge. He saw signs that a snowplow had made a stab at clearing the accumulation from the previous night's storm, but the pass was covered anyway which made for slow going. The chains on the tires dug deeply into the steep grade as they ascended. Even though the top of the mountain was close, a heavy screen of trees nearly obscured the waning sunlight.

"What do Sue and Harold do, exactly?" he asked, more to make conversation than anything else. He wanted to hear her voice.

"Tend to basic maintenance, really. Keep bears and trespassers out. They got married about five years ago and they make a good team." She sighed. "They've been trying to do some improvements since we…since I'm going to sell the place."

There it was in her voice. Defeat. It sickened him. Why did his father's acquisition have to mean defeat for Ava? The thought twisted inside him like a knife. "They've been busy," he said, pointing to a pile of freshly fallen logs above the road. "Cutting down some dead trees."

She didn't answer.

He thought he saw a flicker of movement in the snow just past the fallen pines, so he braked gently, and Stephanie and Tate slowed behind him.

"Must have been a critter," he decided, moving forward again, the engine whining with the effort.

Ava answered her phone which Luca hadn't heard ring.

"Yes?" She listened hard, knuckles white. "What does that mean?"

Luca hoped it was good news.

Ava asked several more questions which let Luca know it was the police on the other end. She disconnected and exhaled. "They called to say they've traced the Taser back to the manufacturer. They should have an answer on who owns it by tomorrow."

"Good," Luca said.

"They've also suspended the recovery efforts at the crash site."

He wasn't surprised. "Meaning that the driver of the snowmobile might be dead and buried under a blanket of snow until the springtime thaw."

"Or he walked away from the crash and left my uncle to die."

Walked away from the crash…and headed up to Whisper Mountain? He tried to refocus on their ongoing hunt. "Steph sent pictures of the pearl earring to Victor. He's probably been up since he received it, researching. If it was owned by the Danson family, Victor will find out."

Ava gave him the ghost of a smile. "I remember him as being the serious type."

"Yeah, driven and smart as they come. I guess that's why he became a heart surgeon while I went for helicopters."

"You liked the shiny machines?"

He laughed. "That and I can't keep still for too long."

Her smile wavered. "Reminds me of my uncle Paul. Always in motion."

He squeezed her hand and she let him for a moment as they drove by another small pile of logs.

This time, the flicker of movement wasn't his

imagination. Maybe it was a man, maybe a woman, but someone fled behind the stack of logs as Luca stopped abruptly, staring into the snow.

"There, I just saw someone right there," he said, stabbing a finger out the window.

When the logs began to tremble he gave the car as much gas as he could, but the snow worked against the spinning tires. Too slow. The logs came loose and rolled down the slope, picking up speed on the way.

Sluggishly, the car moved forward, but it was not enough.

Luca could only stomp on the gas, urging the car forward ahead of the careening logs, praying that Stephanie and Tate saw the oncoming danger.

"Hang on," he shouted to Ava who clutched her seat belt strap with both hands.

The log continued to plunge toward them, gaining momentum on the icy surface.

Luca fought the wheel. Two more feet and they would move alongside a tree. It would be enough to deflect the blow.

The car bucked and shimmied on the snow as sweat beaded on Luca's forehead.

"It's coming too fast," Ava yelled.

She was right, the log was coming on like a missile, directly for the passenger side where Ava sat.

He had only one option left.

Yanking the steering wheel and stomping on the brakes he put the car into a spin. In a dizzying blur the vehicle cooperated, swinging around so the rear end was in line for collision.

He yelled again for Ava to hold on, but his words were lost as the log struck the back of the car so hard that he could feel the metal crumple behind him. Glass exploded into tiny bits.

The log skipped over the top of the hood and continued its insane trip downslope. Luca had no time to relax because his vehicle, crumpled and smashed, was also sliding down the steep slope, heavily peppered with trees. The brakes were useless. No traction. No way to slow the vehicle.

"We've got to jump," he yelled over the sound of the bottom scraping over the ground.

She nodded, face composed, fingers curled around the handle.

A cluster of thick trees swam closer through the blur. Yards away, then feet.

"Now," he yelled.

Ava yanked on the handle and the door opened, letting in a blast of cold air and flying snowflakes. With one more glance at him she leaped from the car.

Relief surged through him as he pulled the driver's side handle.

As the brown tree trunks appeared before him through the cracked windshield, he realized that the angle of the sliding car had piled the snow so tightly against his side that the door was effectively wedged closed.

He held up an arm to shield his face as the car hurtled toward the trees.

TWELVE

Ava found herself on her back in a pile of snow, the breath driven out of her by the impact. She sat up, head spinning in time to see Stephanie and Tate running toward her.

Stephanie helped her up, her eyes scanning frantically. "Where's Luca?"

Tate continuing on down the slope toward the crashed car, slipping and sliding. "The driver's door didn't open," he yelled.

Stephanie stiffened as if she'd been struck, and Ava's breath caught.

They both looked toward the ruined car, now smashed against the rough bark, a waft of smoke emanating from the crumpled hood.

Luca hadn't made it out.

The thought kept running through Ava's mind as they ran to join Tate who was yanking with all his strength on the door. Far away she could hear Mack Dog's muffled barking from inside the other car.

She drew close, felt the terror rising in her stomach. What would she see through the ruined glass? She had a desperate need to look away, to hide her eyes, but her gaze remained riveted to the crumpled metal. If he was hurt…or worse…she could not bear it.

"It's jammed," Tate called, hustling around to the other side. The passenger-side door had slammed shut again but not fully. It took Ava a moment to force her feet into motion.

As he reached for the handle, the women at his heels, a booted foot punched against the door.

"Luca." Ava felt as if she had screamed the word, but it came out no louder than a whisper.

Luca's head and shoulders appeared, face wet with blood. He blinked and shook the glass from his hair. Her vision blurred for a moment, and she blinked away tears.

"Don't you move," Stephanie said. "I'm calling an ambulance."

Luca took a deep breath and winced. "No need for an ambulance, but I'd sure like to talk to the cops about who sent a pile of logs down on us."

Ava felt the breath go out of her, and she was suddenly dizzy. Tate grabbed her elbow. "Easy."

"Are you hurt?" Luca said, wiping at his forehead.

She took a few steadying breaths. "I'm okay. Just trying to take in what just happened." In truth she was so relieved to see Luca safe that it overwhelmed her. She didn't understand why. He wasn't her family, and certainly not a boyfriend. She wasn't sure they qualified as friends. Perhaps it was thinking about another violent death so soon on the heels of Uncle Paul's that made her uncharacteristically weak. Still, her stomach remained wrapped tightly in knots.

Tate peered down at the runaway log which was now wedged against a pile of rocks. "You think someone sent the logs down on purpose?"

"That's exactly what I think," Luca growled.

Against Stephanie's barrage of warnings, Luca got to his feet, sending another shower of glass sprinkling down.

Ava's mind raced. Luca should not be sitting out in the cold, and his wound needed treatment. The weather report spoke of a storm approaching, a big one, and the gathering clouds confirmed it. "The lodge is only about a mile up the road. I think we should head there. Who knows how long before the cops arrive?"

Stephanie agreed, and Tate helped extricate what they could of their baggage. They made their unsteady way back up to the car. Luca accepted a slobbery welcome from Mack Dog, and they piled into the car. Stephanie sat next to Luca in the back, pressing a corner of scarf to his bleeding forehead.

Ava was glad to be in the front with Tate, Mack Dog squeezed at her feet. She did not want to be near Luca now, not until her cascade of emotions settled down. But as they passed the familiar outbuildings and pulled up to the rustic wood-sided Whisper Mountain Lodge, Ava could not ignore the mixture of nostalgia and pain that whirled through her.

Lights glowed softly in the curtained windows and softened the signs of age and neglect. Overgrown pines crowded the roof, the long stone walkway that had not been cleared of snow meandered by the sign hewn by her grandfather out of granite: Whisper Mountain Lodge, Gem of the Sierras.

The irony struck her.

Gems.

Were they the cause of her uncle's death?

The treasure, whatever it was, had cost much more than it could ever be worth. He was gone, and Whisper would be sold. The new owners would probably tear down the old buildings, install modern facilities to offer the newest and best luxuries to visitors.

The door flung open, and Sue Agnoti rushed out.

"Oh, honey. I'm so sorry about Paul. I…" She broke off in midstream as she took in the sight of Luca.

Harold joined her in the doorway, a few inches shorter than Sue, with sparse gray hair and a face seamed by wrinkles. He frowned. "What happened to you?"

"Had a little accident with some logs back on the main road," Luca said.

"Logs? I can't believe that."

Sue elbowed him. "Harold, let them into the house at least." She ushered them in. "This is my husband, and he's got no manners. I'm so sorry. What can we do to help you?" she clucked as she escorted them down the hallway and into the cheerful kitchen where a platter of brownies sat on the kitchen table.

Harold looked Mack Dog over. "Okay to put him outside?"

"No," Ava said. "I'm sorry, but Uncle Paul wouldn't want Mack Dog in the cold."

"That's right," Sue nodded. "He never would see fit to have that dog anywhere but by his side, and he told Harold as much." She sent her husband a disapproving look.

Harold shrugged. "Doesn't seem right to have an animal in our kitchen, is what I told him, but he never listened."

My kitchen. At least for a little while longer. Mack Dog settled himself on the floor with a wary eye on Harold, as if he could read the man's thoughts.

Stephanie forced Luca into a chair. "Cops will come when they can." She shot a look at Ava. "I'm afraid your car is totaled."

Ava sighed. The car was her only vehicle, and she had no idea how to come up with the money to buy another until Whisper finally sold. For some reason, it did not seem to matter much. Luca took the towel Sue offered him and wiped at his forehead. He only succeeded in smearing the blood rather than wiping it away. Ava took the towel from him and pressed it firmly over the wound.

He put his hand over hers. She tried to tell him in that touch what swirled around her heart, the profound gratitude she felt that he was not badly hurt, the flicker of terror she'd experienced when he hadn't gotten out of the wreck in time. And something else, that strange wash of a deeper emotion that she could not name. Instead she said, "That was some good driving," and pulled her hand away.

"Not good enough," he said. "We almost got steamrolled."

Harold's eyes bugged out. "Listen here. I cut and stacked those trees myself. Put wedges in between them and made sure they were dead on steady. No way they rolled down on you."

Luca straightened and winced. "Do I look like I'm making all this up?"

Stephanie took over. "Someone helped the logs along, Mr. Agnoti. Is there anyone working here besides you and your wife?"

"Nah," he said. "Just the two of us."

Ava caught the odd look Sue gave her husband before quickly looking away.

"Just the two of us," Sue echoed softly.

After Ava was settled into a small bedroom in the main lodge, the one her uncle stayed in frequently, the rest of them were installed in a separate little cottage, one that Luca suspected Sue and Harold used to live in when the resort was bustling. An upstairs loft area provided some privacy for Tate and Stephanie while he bunked in a small downstairs room with a window that looked out at the main lodge. A lone rag rug was the only spot of color to liven up the palette of brown cushioned furniture and paneled walls.

Stephanie surveyed the place with a resigned look. "Not four-star, but it's better than the trailer," she said as she headed upstairs to unpack. "At least we convinced Mack Dog to leave Tate and stay with Ava for a while. I was beginning to feel jealous."

The place was musty. Even though it showed some signs of hasty cleaning, it clearly had not been in use for some time.

Harold knocked on the door. When Stephanie let him in, he dropped a paper grocery sack on the counter. "Some supplies. We don't keep much on hand anymore. Just stocked up because the next storm rolling through's supposed to be a bad one."

He turned to go.

"Mr. Agnoti, when was the last time you spoke to Paul?" Luca asked.

Harold turned slowly. "He was here a couple days ago, but I didn't talk to him. Popped in and out over the years since Mrs. Stanton died. Never knew how long he would stay."

"Did you notice him acting strangely? Secretively?"

Harold sighed. "Listen. I'm a simple man. I try

not to get involved in things. If you want to know what Paul was up to, you'd better ask Sue."

"Were they close?"

"At one time they were, a long time ago." A look very like sorrow crossed Harold's face. "Paul was one of those men women like. Good-looking, fancy talker. Charming, is how Sue would put it, I guess."

"And your wife didn't mention anything about Paul's plans?"

He rubbed his forehead. "She doesn't have much to say to me anymore, period." Before Luca could ask anything further, Harold had left, closing the door hard behind him.

Stephanie and Tate joined him.

"Sounds like Harold and Sue are not in the happiest of marriages."

"Too bad," Tate said, putting his arm around her shoulders and kissing her on the temple. "Marriage is the best."

Luca smiled, but he felt a pang in his gut. Tate and Stephanie fit together like two puzzle pieces in spite of their opposite personalities. God brought them together, he was sure, even though they had to go through some horrifying times before they realized it.

He thought about Ava, what she must be feeling staying in the room her beloved uncle so recently made his home. Drifting to the window he looked out on the impossibly perfect mountain peaks, dusted with snow, impervious to the frigid conditions that battered them. Maybe Ava would become like them, hardened by the pain she'd experienced, unable to express the love and gentleness he knew filled her soul deep down.

A light flickered on in her bedroom window. *God, give her some peace,* he prayed.

Luca was staring at his computer screen, eyes burning when the sound of a car pulling up the road brought him to the window. It was not the cops, as he'd expected, but a small sedan. He recognized Charlie Goren immediately as the man struggled free of the car, holding on to his hat against the freshening wind.

Why Goren? Why here? Had he come to express his condolences? Didn't seem like something the nervous little jeweler would do. Stephanie and Tate were getting a walk in before the weather worsened and the sun disappeared. Luca pulled on a jacket and returned to the main lodge.

Sue had settled Goren into a comfortable room which must have served as a recreation spot at some point. Shelves filled with board games lined the walls and jigsaw puzzles almost overflowed a long wooden table.

Goren sat on a sofa upholstered in the same red checkered material as the curtains. Luca wasn't sure how to play it. If the man had come to express his sympathies, then Luca had no business intruding. Ava looked up from her seat near the fire crackling in the old stone hearth. She gave him a small smile and gestured him over.

He moved to a chair. "Hello, Mr. Goren."

The man nodded. "Hello. I'm sorry to intrude." His eyes darted from Luca to Ava. "I'm not sure I should have come."

Sue handed them each a thick mug filled with coffee. "If you were a friend of Paul's, then we're glad to see you," she said, taking a seat on the other side of the hearth.

Goren's face showed evidence of a struggle. Luca guessed "friend" might be too strong a feeling for someone who had cheated Goren.

Harold passed by. He looked at Goren and nodded slightly. "Going to town for batteries and water. Storm will be here tonight."

Sue did not answer and Harold left.

Goren cleared his throat. "I should make this quick with bad weather on the way."

Ava nodded encouragingly. "What did you come to talk about?"

He squirmed. "Well, first I wanted to say I'm sorry. Your uncle was not my favorite person recently, but I didn't want him to die."

She swallowed. "Thank you for that."

"Paul came to my shop, like I told you, and showed me what he supposedly got from the storage space. It took me a while to examine the jewelry." His smile was rueful. "I am very involved in my work once I get started. Anyway, while I worked, Paul made himself at home looking at the books on my shelf while he sat in my rocking chair. I was reading there last night and I found this wedged under the cushion."

He pulled a long scrap of paper from his pocket and handed it to her. "Something he scribbled down, but I'm not sure what to make of it."

Ava took the paper and moved to sit next to Luca, so they could both take a look. Her shoulder, warm from the fire, transferred the heat into his body. He leaned closer, and his arm went around her shoulders before he had thought about it, fitting perfectly as if her body was designed to snuggle next to his. He blinked as Sue stepped in behind them to examine the paper.

Danson, Belgium, 1913, Leuven

"What in the world does that mean?" Sue asked.

Goren sighed. "I've no idea. I thought you might. I believe Leuven is a university in Belgium."

"An old one. It was looted by the Germans." Luca's mind whirled. "So Paul was researching a connection between the Danson family and the university?"

"And we've got a date," Ava added. "1913."

"But what does that have to do with the Sunset Star?" Goren said, rubbing his palms on his pants.

"That's what we're going to find out." Luca looked at Goren. "Okay to keep this?"

Goren shrugged. "Sure." He stood up and ducked his head at them. "Just one thing."

Ava gave him an encouraging nod as she and Luca rose.

"If…if you do find the Sunset Star…" He shook his head. "Never mind."

"What is it, Mr. Goren?"

"If you do find it, could I be in on the discovery?" His eyes shone. "If I could be credited as helping find a gem like that, then…" He shrugged. "It would mean a lot to me, that's all."

Ava clasped his forearm. "Of course. And if we do find it, we'll make sure you get back what you're owed and then some. I promise."

Goren's mouth crooked in a slight smile. "Thank you. I appreciate that."

"Mr. Goren, while you're here, would you mind looking at a set of pearls for me? I've had them for years and I wondered about their value," Sue said.

"Of course," he said, eyes shining. "I'd be happy to." They left together and Luca sidled up to Ava.

"How are you holding up?"

She shrugged. "I'm tired."

"I can imagine." They made small talk for a while, but Luca could see it was an effort for her. Sue and Goren returned, still talking about pearls.

"I'm sorry to tell you they aren't genuine," Goren was saying.

Sue smiled. "That's okay. At least now I know for sure."

Goren crossed to the door, but it opened before

he got there. Sergeant Towers appeared, hair speckled with snow.

He greeted them and jutted his chin at Luca. "I took a look at the logs on my way up. You were lucky you got out of that with only a bang on the head."

Luca saw something in the cop's face that made his nerves jump. "Right, lucky."

Towers's gaze roamed the group. "While you're all here, I've got some news about the Taser." He wiped his boots on the mat and came farther into the room.

"You found out who owns it?" Ava said.

"Yes, we sure did. It's amazing how much information you can glean from a tiny piece of metal. Good thing you picked it up, Mr. Gage."

Luca had the feeling the cop was enjoying his moment in center stage. He did not press, but Ava was not so patient.

"Who does it belong to?" she demanded.

Towers looked around the room before he settled on Goren. "Would you like to tell us about your Taser, Mr. Goren?"

THIRTEEN

Ava watched the color drain from Goren's face. This was the man who had killed her uncle? This quiet, unassuming jeweler whom she had felt sorry for a moment before?

Goren sank down into the chair. "This is not happening. It cannot be happening."

Ava felt Luca's arm circle her shoulders, the fingers squeezing some reality back into her body. *Just listen,* the touch seemed to say. *We'll sort it all out.* She took comfort in the gesture as all eyes turned to stare at Goren, who was now visibly shaking.

"It's mine," he whispered.

Towers adjusted the cuff of his jacket. "The Taser is yours, yes. We have the purchase information. Mr. Goren, did you abduct Miss Stanton's uncle?"

Goren jerked and looked at Towers. "No. The Taser was stolen from my shop."

"There's no police report to that effect."

He shook his head. "I didn't realize it was gone

until later, but there was a break-in. You've got it on your records."

Towers nodded. "You called in a burglary a few days ago. We sent an officer to take a report. Broken glass on the outside door. No major damage inside. The place was rifled, you said, but none of the jewelry was taken, just some petty cash from the register."

"And my Taser," he moaned. "I never should have gotten that thing in the first place, but Paul said…"

"What?" Ava snapped. "What did he say?"

"When he came to me for money to help him buy the storage unit, he said that the contents had to be kept safe, that people would kill for it. He was convinced we were getting our hands on something priceless." Goren snorted. "Of course, he never trusted me to keep the treasure here anyway. I never even got to lay eyes on the contents. He kept it himself, except for a few pieces that he showed me."

Ava exchanged a look with Luca. Hidden under the trailer until he or someone else moved it.

The red-spattered jacket came to mind again. Ava was sure if Paul was going to hide something, he would do it right here, at Whisper Mountain. She pulled her attention back to Towers.

"To be clear, Mr. Goren, you believe whoever broke into your store took the Taser and used it to abduct Paul."

Goren nodded.

"And you didn't call us later on to tell us your Taser had been taken?"

"I didn't see the point," Goren said. "I figured it was gone and got myself an old shotgun for protection instead."

"Do you know what troubles me?" Towers said. "Why go to the effort of an abduction in broad daylight? With the potential for witnesses? Why the urgency?"

Ava thought for a moment. "Because the abductor found out Uncle Paul was meeting me, and the secret would be out of the bag." Her stomach twisted. "So whoever it was knew Paul well, knew he was going to meet me at Melody Lake."

Sue shook her head. "He didn't say anything while he was here about going to meet you. I didn't even know you were in town until I heard about what happened to Paul."

Goren sighed. "I didn't hear anything, either. I'm not sure Paul ever told me one true thing in all the years I knew him."

"I believe he did," Towers said. "He told you people would kill for whatever he found. He was right about that."

A chill wriggled up Ava's spine. She left Towers to go over the particulars with Goren again and escaped to the kitchen. The yellow curtains and the old chipped cookie jar reminded her of her mother. The irony was strong in the cheerful hues she always chose, in such contrast to the dark shadows that she could not shake.

"It's got claws into me, Ava, and I can't get away, no matter what I do."

Would depression take possession of her, too? Ava wondered. Would she see the world through joyless eyes one day? Uncle Paul, for all his bad qualities, had always shown her the bright side of life, the optimistic, wide-eyed wonder with which he viewed things. The world was indeed his oyster, and she was the pearl, or so he'd told her.

Luca cleared his throat. "Ava?"

She grabbed a mug and fixed herself some tea. Tears welled up, but she blinked them away. "Do you think Goren is telling the truth?"

Luca shrugged. "I don't know. The break-in isn't a lie. The police can attest to that."

"Someone knew about our meeting. It could have been someone at Peak Season. Bully maybe? A visitor we don't know about?"

Luca gazed out at the heavy curtain of snow. "Maybe someone had access to his phone and checked his texts."

They watched Towers return to his car and head off slowly into the falling snow.

Sue joined them and fetched a glass of water for Goren. "He doesn't look very good. I think he'd better sit for a while before he tries to drive back."

"Sue, are you sure there wasn't anyone else who

could have heard Paul talk about meeting me? Or gotten hold of his phone and seen the text he sent?"

She scrunched up her face. "There's no one here at Whisper, no one who could have heard." She hurried back out with the water.

"That's not quite right," Ava said, seeing the same conclusion in Luca's face. "There were two people here. Sue and her husband."

"What do you know about Sue?"

Ava thought a moment. "Paul met Sue decades ago when she sang at a concert in Texas, I think. She was really into music and wanted to sing professionally. Paul helped her along for a while and she came with him to Whisper. Mom and Dad hired her on as a caretaker, and she's been here ever since."

"Things between her and Paul didn't work out, I take it?"

Ava sighed. "I thought they would get married. He used to call her his blackbird."

"What happened?"

"I'm not sure. I know Sue has a son. He was a young teen when she and Paul were an item. Uncle Paul always said God didn't give him children for a good reason. I think he was scared of the responsibility. She married Harold a few years ago. He's been working on the mountain for twenty years, and my father trusted him."

"Do you?"

She met Luca's gaze. "I don't know. He was always quiet, reticent almost and never a fan of my uncle. He kept to himself and stayed away from the guests. He can fix anything. He used to keep that horrible old Mack truck Uncle Paul owned running. That's the one thing they could talk about without sniping at each other."

Ava felt suddenly overwhelmed. "Luca, if it is here, this treasure, how am I ever going to find it?"

He flashed her an arrogant smile that made her stomach tighten, just as it had when they were teens.

"Didn't I mention that I'm an expert treasure hunter?"

She smiled back. "I believe you did, but this might be too much even for your legendary skills."

"No way," he said. "I'm invincible."

"That's good to know because we need something going for us right now." She didn't know why she'd used the word *we*. She busied herself rinsing the mug, hoping he hadn't noticed.

"First thing we should do it search his room. That's the obvious place to start."

Sue appeared in the doorway looking frazzled. "We've got a little problem," she said.

Luca crunched out in the snow. It was nearly dusk and the heavy bank of clouds made it even darker. He held a flashlight to Goren's tire.

"Flat, all right."

"Do you have a spare?" Ava asked.

"Doesn't matter," Sue said. "All four are flat."

Luca could not tell exactly how the damage was done, but it was true that all the tires had been flattened.

He looked around, unable to see any footprints, and cast an eye to the tree line. "Has your husband returned yet, Sue?"

"Yes, he got back a few minutes ago." She frowned. "Why do you ask?"

Luca shrugged. "No reason, other than we're going to have to find a place for Mr. Goren to bunk for the night."

"No need for that," Goren said. "Can't someone else drive me back to town?"

"Not in this weather," Luca said. "You're stuck here until morning."

They returned to the lodge, and Luca caught her arm, letting Sue and Goren go ahead. "Ava, I want you to be careful. Don't go out walking around on your own and keep your door locked tonight," he whispered in her ear, the soft strands of hair tickling his cheek. He pressed closer, maybe closer than was strictly necessary. "Something is going on."

"Do you think Harold slashed the tires?" she whispered back. "Why would he do that?"

"I have no idea. It could be someone else, but why? Anger? To keep him here overnight? It makes no sense."

She'd started to shiver, so he guided her inside. "We'll make up the spare room for you, Mr.

Goren," Sue was saying. "It's not more than a cot, really, but it's warm enough. I'll fix us sandwiches and soup for dinner. Will that suit everyone?"

Stephanie and Tate entered in a swirl of snow with Mack Dog trotting behind.

"That's some storm," Tate said.

Luca nodded and gestured for them to follow him into the family room where he filled them in on the police visit and the disabled car.

Tate frowned. "I don't like it."

"Me, neither," Luca said. "Why don't you strong-arm Mack Dog into staying with Ava tonight."

"You got it," Tate said.

Stephanie's brown eyes sparkled. "Victor found some info for us about the Danson family."

"How did he do that so fast?" Ava said.

"Victor is a whirlwind when he's interested in something."

"So what do you have?"

"The Danson family had roots in Belgium. John's great-grandfather worked at the university there as a gardener. While they were there, they came into possession of the Sunset Star."

"How does a gardener get a pearl like that?" Tate asked.

"That's the romantic part," Stephanie said. "He married into a wealthy family. His wife, Elizabeth, was smitten by the humble gardener who left roses on her windowsill every day. The Sunset Star was part of the dowry, you could say. It came along with Elizabeth."

"Anything else?"

Stephanie shifted. "Well, here's the tricky part. When the Germans looted the university, the Dansons apparently fled. The university was leveled, and the library burned as was Elizabeth's family estate. Both her parents were killed. Fast forward twelve years and the next thing we know, the Dansons are installed in a luxurious home in New York which they own along with the estate in California."

Luca frowned. "So where did they get the money for that if they lost everything?"

"Exactly the question," Stephanie said. "Victor thinks they sold the pearl. There's an obscure reference in a French newspaper about a socialite seen wearing a pink pearl brooch around that same time."

Ava groaned. "If they sold it, how would Uncle Paul have gotten it out of the storage unit?"

Luca shook his head. "I don't know. Any ideas?"

"Could be it wasn't really sold. Victor could be wrong."

Luca huffed. His brother was rarely wrong. It was one of the things that he both admired and found irritating at times.

"Okay. Will you stay on it, Steph?"

"Of course," she said. "I'm going to pull an all-nighter. With this storm, it's going to be impossible to sleep anyway."

"What are you going to do?" Tate asked.

Luca exchanged a look with Ava. "We're going to do a little searching after dinner, maybe go through Paul's things if we can find any."

Ava nodded, and he saw the flash of emotion in her eyes. It would be hard for her to face the task so soon after losing him.

Sue called them to the kitchen, and he took Ava's hand.

"I can search by myself if it's too much," he said. He saw her lips tighten, velvet-pink, just as enticing as they'd seemed the first time he met her a decade before. For a fleeting second he wondered what it would feel like to kiss those lips.

"I can do it," Ava said.

He matched her determined stride, still thinking about that kiss.

Dinner was a quick affair although he had to restrain his food snob tendencies. The vegetable soup Sue warmed would have benefited from the addition of fresh rosemary or even a rind of parmesan thrown in for flavor. Good training prevailed, and he ate the soup and sandwich with a smile on his face and a thank-you for Sue. Tate ate two bowls, once again surprising Luca with his ability to cheerfully devour anything put in front of him.

That would serve him well because Stephanie had no idea how to even boil an egg.

Luca helped clear the dishes and found himself handing dirty plates to Goren, who had rolled up his sleeves and set to work in a sink full of water. He didn't encourage conversation, washing methodically and handing the dishes to Luca who dried while the women wrapped leftover food and cleared the table.

Goren seemed lost in thought. Luca figured he was pondering who had disabled his vehicle and why.

Good questions. He'd left a message for Sergeant Towers, but the wind had picked up power, now blowing the snow into swirls of white against the black sky. There was no way anyone was coming up that mountain tonight.

No, it would be just the seven of them, unless someone else was holed up on Whisper Mountain.

He turned to Sue. "Did Uncle Paul have any favorite spots here at the lodge? Any places he frequented often?"

Sue gave him a smile. "Should I call you Sherlock?"

He bowed. "At your service, madam," he said in an unconvincing English accent.

Her laugh was high, mingled with the storm that moaned and screeched outside. "Well, Sherlock, Paul was a roamer. He wandered everywhere, the pine groves, the toboggan run, even climbed up the gondola shed to take in the view. I wouldn't say he favored any one spot, though." A glimmer of sadness crossed her face. "He never settled anywhere for long."

That didn't exactly narrow the search grid any, Luca thought. Stephanie's arched eyebrow told him she'd come to the same conclusion.

Harold finished putting batteries into hefty flashlights and handed one to each of them. "We'll probably lose power. Got a backup generator, but it doesn't kick in right away and sometimes I've got to fiddle with it." He paused. "The basement."

"Come again?" Luca said.

"The basement. Paul spent a lot of time in the basement when he was here."

Luca looked into Harold's hardened face. Was there something unsaid there? Something he was trying to get across without really saying so? The old man turned away and disappeared into the darkened hallway.

"Come on, Charlie," Sue said. "Let's get you settled in for the night." They followed the same path toward the back of the house.

Mack Dog, having finished his bowl of kibble and the piece of cheese Tate had sneaked to him, stretched himself to full length, mouth opened wide in a yawn that showed two full rows of pointy white teeth.

"Smart dog," Stephanie said, stifling a yawn.

She came closer to Luca. "Do you want us to help?" she murmured.

He could see the fatigue on her face. "Tomorrow. We'll poke around for a while and hit it hard in the morning. Okay?"

She pinched his cheek and kissed it. "Who knew Sherlock was such a softie? Good night."

Stephanie gave Ava a quick hug. Luca smiled inwardly at Ava's surprised expression. Stephanie was a hugger by nature, and she obviously had begun to consider Ava a friend, or at least an ally.

That was enough. Once Stephanie took on your cause, there was no stopping her. He felt the swell of pride in his sister. Tate put his arm around her and led her to the door where they donned coats and hats again. Luca kept firm hold of Mack Dog who attempted to follow Tate. "Uh-uh, dog. You're on guard duty tonight."

When they were alone in the kitchen, Luca let Mack Dog go. Ava put a flashlight in the back pocket of her jeans. "Where do we start?"

He considered. "It's late, so we take either the basement or Uncle Paul's room."

She looked away, blinking hard. "Maybe… maybe we could wait until tomorrow to tear apart his room."

He wanted to pull her to him then, to ease the sudden sorrow he saw play across her face. "You bet. I can do a quick tour of the basement before we turn in for the night."

The glow of determination appeared again. "We'll do it together."

Together.

He could not understand why the word warmed a trail inside him.

Easy, Luca. Do your job and leave your feelings out of it.

A treasure was waiting somewhere in the darkened lodge.

He could feel it.

FOURTEEN

Ava tried to remember the last time she'd gone down into the basement. It might have been to fetch several jars of strawberry jam for her mother when she was just a child. She recalled the creak of the steep wooden steps, the scent of mold and some indefinable tang of discarded things, cobwebs, the skitter of tiny mouse feet. Her father had shown up to help her find the jam after a while.

"Why are you afraid of the dark?" he teased. "It can't hurt you."

She did not know then that her father was wrong, dead wrong. Darkness hurt the Stantons plenty. It began with the shadow that crept into her mother's face after she miscarried what would have been Ava's sister. It grew with each passing season, swelled as the lodge fell deeper into debt and burgeoned after the fight when her father had stormed out of the house just before a blown-out tire would leave him paralyzed from the waist down. That same darkness dragged her mother out onto the ice that one wretched evening.

She remembered in her teenage angst yelling at her mother, "Why can't you just be happy? Aren't we enough, Mom?"

That question was answered the day she killed herself. They were not enough, not nearly enough to drive away the persistent grief that lived inside Marcia Stanton.

The dark can hurt you. It hurt us all.

Her skin prickled all over in goose bumps as the cold air wafted up from below. She did not realize her breathing had grown irregular until Luca turned to her, eyes wide in the gloom. He didn't say anything, but she could read the question and his tenderness both pleased and scared her.

Somehow he knew that memories lived down there in that basement.

"Let's go," she said, trying to push ahead of him.

He didn't let her get in front. Flicking on the light switch activated a bare bulb hanging on a string down below. It illuminated only a small patch of damp cement floor some thirty feet below and the rickety wooden steps on which they stood.

Surprisingly, Mack Dog flat-out refused to go down the steps, digging his claws in when she tried to urge him on.

"You're being a big chicken dog," Ava said.

Unperturbed, Mack Dog trotted off to the family room, no doubt to curl up near the embers of the fire.

"Apparently your criticism doesn't mean much to Mack Dog." Luca eased down the steps, the wood groaning under his feet.

"How long has it been since these stairs were shored up?" he asked.

"As far as I know, they've never been repaired and my family's owned this place for forty years."

"Swell." He beamed his flashlight over the steep flight of stairs. "I guess I'd better..." He broke off abruptly as the railing gave way and he toppled off the side of the steps, his flashlight spiraling away into the darkness.

"Luca," Ava cried, peering into the void.

After a moment, there was a loud grunt. "I knew that was going to happen."

She heaved a sigh when she caught sight of his fingers, curled around the edge of the steps, his long frame dangling into the darkness. The drop might not kill him if he fell feet first, but the hard cement floor could certainly crack an ankle or backbone. She grabbed his wrists with both of hers and flattened herself against the step.

Luca wriggled from side to side, with Ava holding on to his wrists as tightly as she could and pulling. The wood creaked under his weight and Ava worried that the whole structure might give way. Slowly he inched up until he was able to swing his foot up onto the steps. With a grunt he hoisted himself over and flopped down next to Ava. They both laid there panting.

"I guess you were right about the stairs," Luca said.

Ava laughed. In spite of everything she could not restrain the bubbling laughter that had no business showing up on that damp basement step. The loss, the disappointment and grief all seemed to vanish. Luca laughed, too, his deep chuckle echoing through the basement. He turned on his side until his face was inches from hers. Going suddenly quiet, he reached out a hand and stroked her cheek, sending tingles rippling along her side. "That's what I like about you," he said. "Your practical side."

She felt her face heat up as his fingers teased her, his mouth so close. He leaned in, closing the gap between them until his lips brushed hers. Warmth flooded her cheeks. Too many emotions crashed into her mind and she yanked away, climbing to her feet.

"We'd better watch our step, then," she babbled, moving on down the stairs. It might have been her imagination, but she thought she heard a sigh from Luca as he got to his feet and slowly followed her down.

Her pulse thundered. What had just happened? There was no room in her heart or mind for the emotions that now danced there. Still, her body seemed electrified by his gentle touch. *Calm down,* she commanded herself. *Find this treasure and then Luca will get what he wants and so will you.*

For one confused moment, she could not remember what it was that she desired. Justice? Closure? Peace?

Love?

No, it was not that. Above all things she never wanted to open herself up to that crippling emotion again.

Ever.

She carefully descended into the basement, Luca falling in behind. The cold increased the deeper they went until she was shivering, her feet like frozen blocks in spite of her boots.

They reached the bottom, a rectangular space with metal shelves stacked neatly with labeled boxes. High up on the wall was a small window that allowed in some starlight thanks to a baffle that kept it clear of snow for the most part. There was nothing to see now as the moon was obscured by a bank of storm clouds.

Ava turned her attention to the shelves. Her father's neat handwriting marched across the cardboard boxes: *blankets, miscellaneous kitchen, furnace filters, tools.* They were precisely stacked, so like her father, former army. In his world everything had a proper place in the grand scheme.

How hard it must have been for him to wrestle with her mother's illness, something he could not manage or change.

And how maddening now that his paralysis left him unable to control even his own body. She regretted her earlier phone conversation with him, her recrimination probably heaped on even more frustration.

She tried to focus. "Okay, Uncle Paul. If you hid something down here, it shouldn't be too hard to find."

Luca retrieved his flashlight, shaking it ruefully. "Busted. Harold isn't going to like that."

"He'd like it less if you had broken your leg in that fall or cracked your skull. Imagine the mess."

He chuckled as he checked over the set of shelves on the far wall. "I get the sense no one comes down here."

"There's probably not much reason to because the resort has been closed down for the past two years."

"That's just wrong. The mountain was meant to be skied."

She felt the same stirring she always did when she pictured herself at the top of a run, the slope spreading pristine and white in front of her, as if she was about to be carried on wings.

She felt Luca looking at her, his face strange in the light from the bare bulb.

"The resort should be opened up again," he said.

"It will be, when it's sold." She could not look at him. "When it's not mine anymore."

"Have you considered a partnership? Leasing out some of your slopes?"

"We considered everything, but we're broke, Luca. People don't want to partner with us, they want to buy us out."

"Maybe you haven't found the right partner yet."

"I'm surprised you haven't tried to take us over because your father owns part of Gold Summit. It would be unbeatable if you absorbed Whisper."

He didn't answer.

She felt the realization settle like a fine powder of snow, sifting into her consciousness. "Luca, why did you come here now? To Gold Summit?"

"Mostly vacationing."

"Mostly?"

He sighed and faced her then, shoulders squared. "The fact is, my father is interested in Whisper Mountain. The real estate agent your uncle spoke to contacted us about the possibility, and we came to take a look and consider our options."

Her heart sank. "You came here to buy Whisper."

He held up his hands. "The agent said you'd decided to sell. We had such fond memories of the place…"

Anger hummed inside her. "So our failure, our bankruptcy is a business opportunity to you. This whole treasure-seeking thing is just a diversion from your real goal."

"No, Ava." His voice deepened. "I'm here to help

you find whatever Uncle Paul left. If it's enough to save Whisper, then I'll be happy."

"Really?" Acid dripped from her words. "Happy to lose out on a once-in-a-lifetime investment?"

He stared at her. "Investments come and go. People are the real treasures."

"That sounds like the sentiment on a greeting card." She bit her lip, finding it hard to breathe.

"I had no idea you'd even be here. I figured you'd have an agent handling the details."

"That would have made it easier, wouldn't it? Why didn't you tell me earlier that you were here to take my property?"

"I should have." His gaze dropped to the floor and he sighed. "I'm not here to take your property. I didn't say anything about the possible purchase because you had your hands full with the abduction, and grieving for your uncle. It did not seem like an appropriate time to bring up business." He moved closer. "I'm sorry. I didn't mean to cause you any pain."

"You should have told me."

"Probably. Sometimes I don't make the right choices, especially where women are concerned. Ava, I'm really sorry."

Me, too.

I thought...

What had she thought? Swirling snow made shadows dance along the cement floor.

It didn't matter. He was right. Whisper Mountain

opened up again, and the Gage family had the money and resources to make it happen.

Luca was just another interested investor.

Swallowing hard, she turned away from him.

Luca ground his teeth. He hadn't lied. And she'd offered the property for sale. It was all perfectly aboveboard, yet he felt a surge of guilt that he hadn't told her sooner. In truth, merging Whisper Mountain with Gold Summit would make it an unparalleled resort experience. On the outside, it made perfect sense.

But from where he stood now, he wasn't sure anymore.

If the Gages didn't buy it, someone else would, someone who had no fond memories of winters past, perhaps an investment group who would raze the place, obliterate any traces of the Stanton family.

He wanted to take hold of her, to make her look into his eyes and see that he was not there in that dark basement on Whisper Mountain for any reason except one: to help her. He thought about the brief moment when his lips brushed hers, the unfettered laughter that lit up her face only moments before.

He took a step toward her when something caught his eye. He went down on one knee and peered into a corner, wishing he had a working flashlight.

Ava joined him, keeping a good couple of feet between them, he noticed.

"Find something?" her tone was cold.

"Aim the flashlight lower." The combined light from the electric bulb and Ava's flashlight revealed a pile of neatly stacked blankets partially covering a wooden trunk. On the outside was scrawled the words *snowshoes*. He might not have thought anything odd about it except that the print was messy, the letter size uneven, different than Bruce Stanton's meticulous handwriting.

He tossed the blankets off the top and pulled the trunk out of the corner. It was about four feet square, well-made.

Luca shot her a look. "It's not locked. Do we open it?"

"Yes," Ava said. "Maybe this treasure hunt will be over, and we can end this thing."

Ignoring the tightening in his stomach, he pulled open the trunk.

Ava beamed the flashlight inside.

This time, the box was not empty.

Luca's heart beat fast as he removed the contents, handing them to Ava.

"An old book, *History of the Printing Press.*" He plunged a hand into the box. "And a bag of…"

Ava beamed her light into the bag. "Jewelry," she announced triumphantly.

He tried to see what was in it, but all he could make out was a tangle of chains. The Sunset Star might very well be dangling in front of his face, wrapped up in an ordinary plastic bag.

...uth was open, eyes searching the con-
...s for the same reason. "Do you think it's in
there?"

"Let's take it upstairs and find out."

She nodded.

"Ava…" He wanted to say something to erase the
distance that had grown between them. Instead, he
shook his head. "I think it would be a good idea to
keep this quiet."

"You don't trust Goren?"

"Or Harold and Sue."

She considered, head cocked. "They've been
with our family for years."

"I know, but someone killed your uncle, and it
had to be someone who knew him well enough to
find out that he'd gotten his hands on a treasure."

"Okay," she said, after a pause.

Another shadow darkened the window, only this
time, it stayed.

Luca jerked. "Someone's looking in over the baffle," he yelled as he sprinted to the window.

As he neared, the glass splintered in all directions. Something metallic sailed through the pane,
showering the cement with brittle shards and
smashing the hanging lightbulb. The bulb sparked,
and the basement went black.

FIFTEEN

Ava felt fragments of glass whiz by her face before she ducked away. Luca crunched frantically across the littered floor, searching for the flashlight she'd dropped. She found it first and clicked it on. His face was intense in the strange light. Angry.

He ran to the steps and took them two at a time. "What are you going to do?" she called after him.

He didn't answer, just barreled out the basement door. After a moment, she followed. She topped the stairs in time to see Mack Dog's tail disappearing out the kitchen door after Luca.

The storm hit her like a backhanded slap as she emerged outside, snow pricking her cheeks. Because her jacket remained on the hook by the fire, she was instantly chilled. The black night swirled around her, and it suddenly came home that somebody had broken the window, hurling a heavy object through that might have crashed into either one of them.

Shadows from her own light picked out sinister

shapes, moving trees, windblown pockets of snow. No Luca.

Getting her bearings she headed for the window where Luca would have gone.

He wasn't there. Neither was Mack Dog.

She looked out into the angry storm. Hurt as she was that Luca hadn't been forthright with her about buying Whisper, another emotion rose to the top. Where had he gone? Dressed as he was in regular clothing, he would not last long in the storm. Disorientation could render a person lost in moments.

She remembered one winter blizzard that hit Whisper smack in the middle of peak season. A young man, showing off for his buddies, insisted on hiking from the family lodge to the lockers where he had left his phone.

Thirty minutes later Ava's father and Harold were out combing the area for him. Forty minutes later they found him, unconscious after running into a tree branch. Nearly frozen, he'd barely survived. Forty minutes could be a lifetime in these conditions.

"Luca," she shouted, but the wind snatched it away.

She checked the snow around the broken window. There might have been some footprints, but her light was not strong enough to help her draw any conclusions from the blurry imprints.

"Luca," she yelled again.

Mack Dog suddenly appeared, bounding over to Ava and poking at her with his nose.

"Where's Luca?" she asked, teeth chattering.

Mack Dog wagged his tail. She shone her flashlight around in the darkness wondering again who had been out here in the storm watching them. Mack Dog barked, startling Ava so badly she dropped the flashlight. Floundering around in the snow she screamed as a cold hand brushed her cheek.

She bolted upright, lashing out at her attacker.

A light blinded her.

"It's just me, honey. What are you doing out here?" Sue asked, eyes wide.

Ava's heart slowed a fraction. "Looking for Luca," she said.

Sue puzzled it over. "You've got to get inside."

"I'm not leaving until we find him."

"I'll get Harold. Please come inside and put on a jacket," she said.

Ava shook her head.

"Now you listen to me, Ava Stanton," Sue snapped. "Your father would not tolerate this foolishness and you know it."

"He's not here," she shot back, knowing she sounded like an angry teen.

"Don't you say that. He'll be back soon as he's able," she said, lips trembling. "You know he trusted me to be in charge, and I won't let him down. Inside, right now."

Ava was so surprised at Sue's emotion that she followed her back toward the house. Sue was wearing a pair of sweats and a long-sleeved shirt with a jacket pulled over it, boots on her feet. Much more sensibly dressed than Ava whose teeth chattered violently. She would grab her jacket and return to the search.

Ava stopped before they reached the kitchen door and turned to peer through the storm.

A light appeared in the darkness, illuminating a slice of falling snow as it bobbed side to side. A flashlight. She tensed.

Mack Dog barked again and took off toward it.

Ignoring Sue's strong protest, Ava ran back out into the storm. It had to be Luca. It had to be.

"Luca?" she called.

"Nope, Tate." Stephanie's husband limped into view. "What's going on? Couldn't sleep, and I heard barking."

Ava's heart dropped. "Luca's out here somewhere."

Tate didn't ask why. "Let's split up. I'll take the woods. You scan the perimeter of the house, stay with Sue."

"She should come inside, and we'll wake up Harold," Sue insisted as she joined them.

Tate was about to respond when a window slid open from the second floor. "What's happening?" Goren called out. "Is someone hurt?"

"No," said a deep voice, thick with irritation.

That one syllable flooded Ava's heart with relief.

Luca trudged out from a thicket of pines, shivering and angry. "I'm fine, and whoever broke the window must be, too, because I couldn't catch him. He got away from me."

"Happens to the best of us," Tate said, clapping him on the shoulder and shoving him toward the lodge.

Ava could not restrain a smile at the look of fury on Luca's face. She knew it came more than anything from the fact that he'd been outrun. She'd seen similar expressions on his face when they were kids and she beat him down the mountain. Every time.

She let him go first so he would not detect her own deep sense of relief. Luca was okay and at the moment, that carried more weight than anything else.

Once inside, Luca could not be persuaded to sit down. He headed immediately to the basement. "We should have secured the stuff. Stupid of me to take off like that."

"What stuff?" Sue called from the top of the stairs.

Ava was going to call up and explain when Luca let out a grunt of rage.

A heavy metal pipe lay on the floor amid a cascade of glass.

Nearby, the wooden trunk lay empty.

Ava held the flashlight as Tate made his way painfully down the basement stairs to join them.

Their search netted nothing. Luca smacked a fist on the wall in frustration. "Guy came back while I was chasing shadows. It was just a ruse to get us out of here."

When Ava could stand the cold no longer, she headed up the stairs and straight for the fireplace. Goren and Sue stood wide-eyed.

"The suspense is killing me," Sue said. "What did you find in that trunk?"

"Was it the Star?" Goren breathed, quivering with excitement. "Did you find the Sunset Star?"

Luca accepted a blanket from Sue and stood near the fire. "Not sure. We found a bag of jewelry and a book, but we didn't get a chance to look thoroughly."

"The pearl might have been reset onto a pendant or a brooch. Did you see anything like that?" The firelight made Goren's face younger, childlike.

"I'm not sure." Luca sighed gustily. "Now we might never know."

Sue shook her head. "I can't believe any of this. I figured this treasure was just another one of Paul's daydreams." She laughed. "That was the very best thing about Paul. He could make you believe in the impossible."

Ava's heart squeezed. "Yes," she said softly, "he certainly could." Luca took a step toward her, as if he meant to give her a comforting embrace, but he stopped abruptly.

She steeled herself against the unwelcome swirl of disappointment. *No comfort from Luca Gage, Ava.*

"We're all half-frozen. I'm making some tea," Sue said as Harold joined them, cheeks flushed. He was fully dressed, Ava noted, though she saw no sign that he had been out in the storm. She felt guilty for her suspicions.

Harold was the man who built ramps after her father was paralyzed, converted the bathroom with wider doors and lower fixtures to accommodate the wheelchair. He'd never complained about the extra work, never asked for more salary although she knew they did not pay him much. The only time she'd seen him emotional at all was the day he married Sue in a civil ceremony with only Ava and her father in attendance. It was a run-down, dingy room in the town hall, but it might have been the Notre Dame Cathedral for all the pride she saw in his face that day.

Sue took Harold into the kitchen with her with promises to fill him in, and Goren returned to his room, muttering softly to himself on the way.

Tate looked up from scratching Mack Dog's neck. "Any ideas who busted the window?" he said, voice low.

Luca frowned. "Could have been any of them or none of them. Whoever I was chasing was quick, that's about all I can figure. He doubled back around into the house after I lost him and headed straight for the basement."

Tate nodded. "Maybe Victor can do some digging about all three of them. Find out how this all fits together."

Ava flushed. "No."

Both men looked at her.

"Someone is trying to steal from you and they're not afraid to hurt you in the process," Luca said. "We've got to figure out which one of these three it is."

"Sue and Harold were my mother's friends. They love me and they'd never do anything to hurt me."

"Maybe you don't know them as well as you think."

"I know them better than you," she fired back.

Tate considered. "If Harold and Sue are out, does that mean you think Goren is our guy?"

Ava shrugged. "I don't know. The police are already investigating him, but I'm not going to have the Gages prying into the Agnotis' lives. It's not right."

"I know they're like family," he said quietly, "and that's a difficult subject right now."

A difficult subject? It was the only subject that mattered anymore. Her uncle was gone and her mother, too. All she had left was her father and she was about to lose Whisper, the one place that held all her most precious memories. All the love that had once thrived here mingled with the sorrow that still circled like the winds that cradled the mountain. "They are good people."

"Are you're afraid of what you'll find out?" Luca asked softly.

She felt her self-control splintering. "Well, maybe I am afraid. I guess that makes sense because I'm the daughter of a woman who jumped in a lake rather than face her problems." Tears crowded her eyes, mortification at her outburst flooded through her.

Luca opened his mouth but nothing came out. He tried again. "Ava, I'm…"

She waved him off. She could not stand to see pity on his face, pity for the little girl whose mother had abandoned her in the worst possible way. She would not be seen as a victim. Not by Luca, especially not by him.

She turned to face him, chin high, when Sue poked her head in. "Tea will be ready in a minute."

Tate thanked her and begged off. "I'm not a tea guy," he said. "Besides, Stephanie will have my head if she wakes up and finds out I went wandering. I've got some explaining to do about why I didn't include her in all the fun."

He left. The silence thickened around them.

Luca shrugged off the blanket Sue had draped him with and offered it to her.

"No, thank you," she said, stiffly.

"I am sorry things are working out this way." He paced back and forth. "I don't want to make you uncomfortable or pry into personal business."

"Then don't," she said, arms wrapped around her.

"You can't just walk away from this," he said as the kettle whistled in the kitchen.

"Maybe I can." She looked around the lodge, the warn draperies, the puzzles that had gone untouched for years. "I can contact the agent in the morning. I'll sell to the highest bidder, maybe even your father, and walk away."

He sighed. "Is that what you really want? To leave it all behind?"

She felt a myriad of feelings, joy and sorrow, fear and nostalgia tumbling together through her heart. "I don't know." The tears came suddenly, and before she knew it she was in Luca's arms. He didn't speak, stroking her back, his chin resting on the top of her head.

"If you need to leave, to get out of here for a while, do it." His murmurs tickled her ear, tracing a path of electricity through her torso.

With great effort she pulled away. "And would you make the same choice? Leave the treasure behind?"

He paused. "No."

She stiffened. "So that is really why you're here. It's all about the treasure."

"No, Ava. You know it's not true."

She struggled to keep from crying. "You're a treasure hunter and that's the bottom line."

His eyes sparked. "Bottom line? Here it is. Someone murdered your uncle. Walk away if you have to, Ava, but you can't leave that truth behind. If someone finds that treasure before we do, they get away with causing your uncle's death." He groaned, closing his eyes for a moment. "Who am I kidding? They might have already because I left that trunk. Easy pickings."

Ava's resolve toughened inside her. He was right, although she still suspected the treasure and Whisper were his bigger motivations. Whoever killed Uncle Paul would not go unpunished as long as she was alive. If vengeance was the only reason to stay here at Whisper, then so be it.

"Okay. If the treasure is the key, then I've got something for you."

Luca's eyebrows arched. "You do?"

She pulled the bag of jewelry from her sweatshirt pocket. "I grabbed it before you took off."

He gaped. And then he took her in his arms and planted a kiss on her temple. "I couldn't have done it better myself."

"You're right," she said, heart pounding.

SIXTEEN

Luca still had his arms around Ava when Sue cleared her throat discreetly. He let Ava go, watching her eyes shift from looking at Sue over his shoulder to him. He could see the struggle there. She trusted Sue and Harold. She did not want to hide things from them.

He hoped she could read his expression. *Your call.*

In the end, she stuffed the bag back into her pocket, while Luca's body still blocked Sue from seeing. How hard would it be if these people she loved turned out to be killers? He breathed a silent prayer that it would not come to that, and he and Ava joined the two in the kitchen where they sipped some flavorless tea.

Luca could hardly contain his eagerness to leave, to go and examine the contents. Instead, he forced himself to contribute to the discussion.

"The pipe that busted the window belongs in the garage," Harold said.

"Well, don't move it," Sue advised. "The police might want to check for prints and such, or maybe I just watch too many crime shows on TV."

"No, you're right. It's a good idea to leave it," Ava said.

Sue sipped her tea. "You sound just like your father. Practical and pragmatic. How is he? Did the surgery go well?"

Ava was surprised that Sue knew the details of her father's recent procedure. "Yes, it went fine. He's recovering and we hired a nurse. I would have stayed, but he wanted me to move the sale forward."

She looked stricken. "Don't say that, Ava. It doesn't have to be that way. We can turn things around here at Whisper. I know it."

"Now you sound like Paul," Harold said.

"There are worse things than a little optimism. Bruce just needs to recover and he'll feel differently about selling."

"The resort is in my name now, Sue," Ava said gently. "I've got to make the best decision for me and Dad."

Harold thunked his mug on the table. "She's right. Bad luck is cumulative, like the snow. Couple of bum turns, like lean snow years and expensive repairs, and you get further and further into a hole. Pretty soon you can't dig your way out."

Bum turns, Luca thought, was an understatement. Marcia's suicide on the heels of Bruce's accident.

"So you agree we should sell?" Ava asked.

He shrugged. "Not my call, just seems poor sense to watch the money go down that hole with every passing year. I tried to tell Paul that. When he was poking around up in the gondola I told him it would take thousands to make that thing safe to use again, and that's only the tip of the iceberg, of course."

"I'm surprised Uncle Paul went up there at all," Ava mused. "He's…he was, terrified of heights."

Harold continued as if he hadn't heard. "There are runs to be maintained, the heating system is older than I am and people don't want to stay in a run-down lodge."

Sue took Ava's hands, mouth tight. "I feel so bad about everything. I don't want you to lose Whisper, too."

Luca shifted. If he had known this piece of ground meant so much to Ava, would he have advised his father buy the property? But wouldn't she rather the resort go to people she knew than strangers?

He looked at the determined lines of her profile. Maybe it was too hard to think about the Gage family taking over what her own had failed to hang on to. Pride was a tricky thing. He was not sure he would feel any differently in her place if it was his family that needed bailing out. Still, part of him was pained that she'd painted him as an opportunist.

Finally, they finished the seemingly endless discussion and Harold and Sue trundled off to bed. Luca and Ava waited until the house had quieted again and bundled up to head for the cabin where he was not surprised to find Stephanie awake interrogating Tate about the evening's events.

Luca gave Mack Dog a pat and made sure the curtains were tightly closed before and he and Ava sat around the well-worn coffee table.

"New developments," Luca said, as Ava poured the jewelry out of the plastic bag onto the table. He enjoyed the openmouthed stares of his sister and brother-in-law and the impressed looks they gave Ava when they heard how she'd had the presence of mind to pocket the gems.

"Excellent," Stephanie said, reaching for the jewelry. She sorted it into piles first, three necklaces, a cameo pin, a few rings and the object that made them all squeeze closer, a brooch about the size of a half dollar with a fat pink pearl set in the middle.

His heart hammered. This was it, the treasure that would save Whisper and perhaps point them to Paul's killer.

Stephanie fetched plastic gloves from the first aid kit and set to work examining the items. "It's too dark in here, I'm going to move to the kitchen where the light is better."

Luca followed close on her heels.

She shot him an exasperated look. "You're crowding me. I'll holler as soon as I've come to any conclusions."

"But…"

"Go away, brother," she said.

He huffed and returned to the family room, throwing himself down on the sofa next to Ava who he noticed looked just as anxious as he felt.

"What doesn't make sense to me is why such a big box for a small bag of jewelry and a book? And the box under the trailer was pretty big, too."

"What happened to the book?" Tate asked as Mack Dog came over and bumped against Tate's leg in search of a friendly scratch.

"I forgot all about that," Ava said. "It was gone when we got back to the basement. What was the title again, Luca?"

"Something about the history of the printing press." He frowned. "What does that have to do with a priceless pearl?"

"Maybe it doesn't have anything to do with it," Ava suggested. "It was in the materials Uncle Paul got in that storage unit. Coincidental."

"Why hide it, then?" Tate stroked Mack Dog's ears, and the dog subsided into a contented puddle at his feet.

"Good question." Luca turned it over in his mind, interrupted when his sister called from the kitchen doorway.

"Well," Stephanie said. "Maybe because the book was worth more than this jewelry."

They stared at her.

She leaned on the jamb, a look of irritation on

her face. "It's costume jewelry. Nice stuff, but not anywhere near priceless."

"Are you sure?" Ava asked.

Stephanie's lips quirked. "Yes. The metal is actually gold-plated and the stones are manufactured."

"The pearl?" Ava's eyes still held the embers of hope.

"You can ask Goren for his opinion, but it doesn't warm to the touch like a real pearl. It's way too light and too round. Real pearls never have perfect shape or texture."

Ava stood with a groan. "So why all this effort to hide things under his trailer and in the basement?"

"We're missing something." Luca knew it deep in his gut. He took out his phone and dialed Victor's number.

"It's after one o'clock in the morning," Stephanie chided.

"The guy sleeps only four hours a night. I'm sure he's gotten his beauty rest by now." Indeed, Victor sounded completely alert when Luca put him on speaker phone.

"Did I wake you?"

"Haven't gone to bed yet. I've been researching John Danson's great-grandpa."

Luca smiled. That was the brother he knew, the one who earned the nickname Sea Tiger, or barracuda, for his tenacity. Luca brought him up to speed on their find of the book and worthless jewelry. "So tell me you've got something that will enlighten us."

"I'm not sure you'll be happy about this info, but I think I can say without too much doubt that the Dansons did sell the Sunset Star."

Luca felt his breath come out in a whoosh. "How can you be sure?"

"Because the family that bought it donated it to a museum along with an anecdotal history that proves it was the Sunset Star."

The room fell into silence.

Ava closed her eyes. "So that's that. There is no treasure to be found here. Whoever kidnapped my uncle was mistaken. He never had the Sunset Star in the first place."

The look of defeat on her face twisted his gut. "Maybe not, but Paul found a treasure, something bigger than a pearl, so big he went to great lengths to hide it."

She perked up. "Do you really think so?"

Did he? Or was he clutching at straws to give her hope? Was he letting the growing feelings he had for Ava mess with his logic?

Stephanie took up the threads. "Goren already told Paul the jewelry was fake."

"But the kidnapper might not have known that."

Stephanie twisted a strand of her dark hair. "The morning he met you at the slopes. He knew someone was after him, but he also knew that the jewelry wasn't the big score. Then we consider the size of the box he hid, the one under the trailer and the trunk. Much too big for just a bag of jewelry. And the book. Printing presses. Victor, what do you know about early printing presses?" she called.

"Not a thing," he said, "but I'll be an expert in a couple of hours."

"It can wait until morning," she said with a smile. "Go to bed or Brooke will be worried about you."

"In a bit," he said, and they heard the tapping of a keyboard.

Stephanie said goodbye and Luca clicked off the phone.

"I hope you're happy," she said. "He won't get to bed until morning."

Luca laughed. "My bad. Maybe we should all stay up until morning and see what we can dig up."

"Absolutely not," Stephanie said. "Look at Ava. She's exhausted."

It had not escaped Luca that Ava's eyes were shadowed and her shoulders slumped, but he'd always thought action was the best way to fend off fatigue and more importantly, a feeling of helplessness. Now that he looked closer, he knew his sister was right. Ava needed rest. He mentally chided himself when he realized it was morning.

Stephanie continued. "Because we've got some crazy person breaking windows in the main house, Ava is going to bunk with me upstairs and you two manly men can sleep down here with the dog. Turn off the lights and get some shut-eye."

"Yes, ma'am," Luca said. After Stephanie had gone, he laid down on the lumpy couch. "Your wife is one stubborn woman," he said into the darkness.

"She learned it from her brothers," Tate said.

There was one thing Stephanie was right about, Luca thought, as he tried to force his brain to turn off: Uncle Paul had found something big, something worth killing for.

Ava tried not to thrash around on the bed and disturb the peacefully sleeping Stephanie. She did fall into a troubled slumber for a few hours until she jerked awake, thoughts chasing each other through her head. She slipped from under the covers and went to the window, staring out into murky darkness, still hours away from sunup, as she thought about the bag of jewelry. Uncle Paul had been so convinced he'd found a treasure. She desperately did not want him to have risked his life for something worthless.

She remembered the glow in his eyes when he met her at Melody Lake.

"I come here to pray all the time and you used to, didn't you, Ave?"

She hadn't prayed much at all since her mother had breathed in the frigid water that snatched her life away. Long lonely years had followed, hauntingly quiet like snow falling in a silent wood.

Now there was another person gone, another soul whom she had clung to ripped away.

Ava listened to the wind whispering against the windows, startled by a realization. Even though her heart felt cleft in two by grief, mourning her lost uncle, she did not feel alone in that moment.

She wrapped her arms around herself. The feeling made no sense. Paul was dead. Her mother gone. Her father crippled and likely never to return to Whisper. There was no one here for her, yet she had the odd sense that she was not alone.

"...you used to, didn't you, Ave?"

She'd prayed with her mother here as the seasons changed in all their splendor, prayed the few months after her death.

Don't leave me alone, Father.

She pictured Luca, laughing, sprawled on the basement steps.

Could those prayers have been heard, she wondered? Had her desperate lonely cries risen into the exquisite mountain air, biding time until the Lord answered them?

The notion tantalized her for a moment, warming a place deep inside her soul until the coldness returned. Luca was a temporary distraction and what's more, he was here to acquire Whisper, a fact he'd failed to mention. She felt an ache, deep down.

You are alone, Ava. There could be no comfort here in the place where she had lost so much. Luca would soon be gone and the silence of Whisper Mountain would return to smother her again.

SEVENTEEN

She prowled the room, picking up her phone to check the storm's progress. When the weather cleared, the police would return and perhaps be able to figure out who had slashed Goren's tires and broken the basement window. It all seemed so pointless, like acts of a rebellious teenager.

She was surprised to find a message on her phone from Sergeant Towers. Even though she'd been expecting the news, she felt a surge of nausea.

Uncle Paul's body had been released.

She could put it off no longer. It was time to arrange for a final goodbye. It wouldn't be fancy, Sue had helped her make some initial arrangements. A small memorial ceremony after a private funeral. Her father was too ill to come even if he wanted to. It would probably be only herself and Sue in attendance.

A pitifully small goodbye for a larger-than-life man. She still expected him to burst through the door at any moment, red cap on his head and a wild plan on his lips.

Her phone showed that it was nearly five, too late to go back to sleep and too early to expect anyone else to be up. She made up her mind to slip back to the lodge and search her uncle's room. From there she could make phone calls to finalize the details of her uncle's memorial service.

Quietly she left the bedroom and made her way to the kitchen.

The smell of garlic sizzling in butter greeted her.

She was startled to find Luca there, a towel thrown over his shoulder as he stirred the pan on the stove, adding red peppers before pouring beaten eggs over the contents.

He looked up when he heard her. "Sorry. Did I wake you? Tate could sleep through an air raid siren, so I figured my cooking wouldn't annoy him."

She shook her head, amused at the sight of this husky man working culinary magic. "What are you cooking?"

"Frittata."

"That trumps my scrambled eggs."

"Your eggs were great." He tossed a handful of herbs and sprinkled it all with salt. "I went over to the main house and swiped stuff from the fridge."

"You're not up for one of Sue's toast and tea breakfasts?"

He chuckled. "I'm a food snob, or so my sister

will tell you. When I stay at my dad's house, I annoy the cook endlessly by bullying my way into the kitchen and taking over. She's threatened to quit before."

Ava could not restrain a laugh as she watched him ease the frittata over after the bottom had cooked a bit.

She felt him looking at her. "Something wrong?"

"No, I just forgot the sound of your laugh. Kind of sweet and rolling. I remember hearing it when we used to come and ski here." He looked back at the pan. "I used to listen for it when you were out showing the guests around. That's how I'd find you."

Her eyes widened. "Is that why you always seemed to join in my guided tours?"

"Yes, ma'am." He tossed a handful of Swiss cheese over the top. "I prefer Bergenost cheese, but that's just my inner snob talking."

"Why?"

"Why the cheese?"

"No." She swallowed. "Why did you come find me all those times?"

"Well, at first it was probably because of the most obvious shallow teen criterion."

"What's that?"

He cocked an eyebrow. "You don't see it, do you?"

"See what?"

"That you are gorgeous."

Her cheeks flooded with heat. "Me?" she squeaked. "No, I guess I never have."

He shrugged. "Maybe that was part of the other reason. You had this spirit about you, a sort of open genuineness is the best way I can say it."

She dared not look at him. Her stomach was tumbling over itself. She had never heard anyone say such things. "I'm glad I seemed that way to you. That was a long time ago."

"Hasn't changed." He shot her a look, eyes filled with warmth that tickled something deep down inside her.

She jerked. "I…I'm not the same person I was at sixteen."

"Nobody is." Luca slid a mug full of fragrant coffee in front of her. "You're not supposed to be."

She looked deep into his green gaze, wondering what she looked like to him. He saw something that she did not. It both thrilled and scared her. She drank a slug of coffee, burning her mouth in the process.

"So…I just figured I'd, um, go search Uncle Paul's room."

The expression on his face made her think he wanted to talk about an entirely different subject, but she plowed ahead anyway. "I don't think anything's hidden there, but it's something to do while we're stuck here. I need to make some phone calls to plan Uncle Paul's service, but nothing is open this early, of course."

He took the frittata out of the oven and cut a wedge for her, a pool of melted cheese oozing over the edges onto the plate. The fragrance made her mouth water.

"I think we should eat breakfast first," he said. "Then, I've got a wild idea to run by you."

Luca sighed inwardly. He'd made her uncomfortable, that much was certain. He shouldn't have shared his memories. Big mouth, no filter. She'd eaten the frittata and let him detail his nutty idea. At least that gave them something to talk about that put her back on safe ground.

The gondola.

The old monolith that stood sentry over the mountain, the one Paul had been interested in in spite of his fear of heights.

He could not get it out of his mind. Why would Paul climb up that rickety ladder in the first place unless he'd had a very good reason?

"Let's go find out," Ava said, taking her plate to the sink.

They donned jackets and headed out into the snow, snowshoes in hand. An exquisite sunrise greeted them, showering gold and orange through the patchwork of clouds. For a moment they both stood there staring. He felt the divine majesty of the place sweep through him. He wondered if Ava felt it, too.

The storm had died away, leaving Whisper

Mountain buried under three feet of new snow. It would be several hours before they would get a plow to clear the road so they could head back to town. Hopefully the police had spent the time investigating all possible leads. As far as he knew, the coroner's preliminary finding had been Paul died of head trauma probably due to the wreck and exposure, none of which helped point toward his killer.

As he strapped on his snowshoes, he felt a growing sense of urgency. Until they found this treasure, he had the strong sense that Ava's life would be in danger and the thought of her getting hurt burned like strong poison inside him. He hurried, trying to keep up with Ava's brisk pace and superior snowshoeing ability.

The bottom tower nestled at the foot of a slope a good two miles from the guest lodge. The single cable stretched up the mountain, terminating at the top tower. The gondola itself rested in the bottom tower, parked in the rectangular shed where passengers would board before their thrilling ascent.

It must have been a jewel of its kind twenty years ago. Now, Luca knew, lift systems had gone high-tech featuring enclosed cabins that could carry up to sixteen passengers. This old setup featured a rustic two-seater gondola that would meander its way to the mountain top, disgorge passengers and make its leisurely way down the mountain. It was a relic from days gone by, but there was something special about it anyway.

He knew because he'd ridden it many times during those long-ago winters. He and Ava had crammed in it a time or two, skis balanced on their laps, predicting who would be the first to make it back down to the lodge. The Stantons did not have the money to replace the hopelessly out-of-date gondola, nor did they have the money to have it removed, he guessed. So it sat, victim of the elements, standing sentry over the silent slopes of Whisper Mountain. He tried to get a glimpse of Ava's face to see if she was feeling the same sense of nostalgia, but she'd moved ahead, reaching the metal-sided shed, perched on a network of pipes that held it above the ground. Because it had been a lean snow year, they would have to use the ladder welded to the side to reach the shed.

"Maybe," Ava said as she unbuckled her snowshoes, "Uncle Paul hid something inside the shed. He wouldn't like climbing the ladder, but if there was a good enough reason, he might have considered it."

Luca followed suit. "Could he have been trying to figure out what it would take to bring the lift back up to par? Inspecting the gondola itself maybe to get some sense of the investment required?"

Ava laughed. "Uncle Paul would not have set foot near that gondola. He thought it was a death trap even back when it was in perfect working order. If he hid anything there, it'll be in the shed."

She climbed quickly and he did the same. The

ladder seemed sturdy under his grip, patches of rust not having caused too much damage. As they ascended he turned his head to look down. The lodge and guesthouse were concealed by the swell of the slope, the ground swaddled in a new layer of snow.

"Ava," he called up to her, "do you see that?"

She stopped and peered in the direction he was pointing.

"Under the trees, you mean?"

"Uh-huh," he said slowly. Somewhat sheltered from the previous evening's deluge, the ground at the foot of a massive pine showed a distinctive imprint along with a furrow leading away from it that promptly lost itself in the deeper snow.

"Snowmobile," Ava said.

He nodded, wondering who had been prowling around the property on a snowmobile in the throes of a winter storm. Were the tracks from last night? This morning? He'd not even seen a snowmobile in the garage during his search for the person who threw the pipe into the basement.

"Does your family keep one on the property?" Luca said as he topped the ladder, stepping into the dark interior.

"We had one years ago, but Uncle Paul wrecked it and we never had the money to replace it. I never heard Harold or Sue mention that they owned one."

"And Goren wouldn't have had any way to get his hands on one unless he parked it here on some previous occasion."

"Could be a trespasser. We get them all the time. People looking for that perfect slope."

He nodded and did not pursue the matter, but his gut told him this particular trespasser was not in search of a good ski run. Perhaps Goren, Sue and Harold were not the only people involved.

Because the shed had no windows, it was almost completely dark inside. Luca switched on his flashlight and beamed it over the frigid interior. The periphery of the space was stacked with a variety of things from tall boxes to an old gondola set on its side. The more serviceable gondola was perched on the floor at the edge of the opening that looked down on the panorama below. It was attached to the steel cable by a crooked arm, the acceleration controlled by the operator who stationed at the dust-covered levers tucked into the corner. Definitely old-school.

"This place has seen better days," Luca said.

Ava moved to the opening, gazing across the rippling topography of Whisper Mountain. "Yes, but what a view. My dad used to take us up here, and my mom and I would get a private ride. My mother used to say I was the only girl in the world who owned her very own mountain."

He saw the gleam of tears in her eyes and he took her hand. "You had some good times here."

She nodded. "Sometimes I forget. Mom's death sort of drove the sweet memories away." She sighed. "It's nice to remember for a minute."

He squeezed her fingers and resisted the sudden urge to press them to his lips as they stood there looking out at the white world below them.

I'm not the same person I was at sixteen.

You're better, he wanted to tell her. *You're just as breathtaking inside and out as this view.*

After a moment, she gently took her hand from his and reached for the lever on the gondola roof. The little door slid open with a squeal and a strong smell of rust. "Might as well check here, too, because we came all this way."

She shone her own flashlight under the seats, bending to peer closer. "Just a coil of rope and an old screwdriver. I don't see any evidence that my uncle was even up here. Maybe Harold was mistaken."

Luca looked over her shoulder and concurred. The old metal seats were covered with moisture and a patch or two of mold. It looked as if nothing had been touched for years. "I told you it was a wild idea," he said without much enthusiasm.

He felt a rush of air. Something hard and long smashed into his head from behind. He toppled forward carrying Ava down into the gondola with his weight. He felt the lurch of movement and his eyes were dazzled by a sudden onslaught of sun. He struggled to right himself, but found he could not get any leverage in the tiny space.

There was a dizzying sense of the floor rocking underneath him.

The reality finally hit home as the gondola sped out along the ancient cable, heaving violently from side to side.

EIGHTEEN

Ava struggled to breathe with Luca's heavy weight on top of her. The spiraling sensation in her stomach told her that they were falling.

Not falling, she realized.

Rising, skimming upward along the cable, the old filament of steel that had been lying neglected for a decade. She could not get her eyes to focus as the world blurred around her.

Luca finally struggled to his knees, a dazed look on his face.

"What happened?" she said after she got a breath.

"Someone hit me from behind."

They both looked out the back window as a bundled figure hurried down the ladder. There was no time to worry about it as the gondola was still jerking forward, shuddering so hard that Ava feared the metal contraption would fall apart.

They were traveling away from the tower at a fast pace, the distance from the ground now a good twenty feet and increasing with every moment.

Fear knotted her insides as the gondola pitched and heaved. She clung to the seat.

Luca tried to get to his feet, but the movement caused the car to swing even more violently, so he quickly returned to his knees. He looked at the cable overhead, and she knew he was thinking the same thing she was. Would it hold?

If it did, they would arrive at the far tower safely and be able to climb down, none the worse for wear. If it didn't…

She closed her eyes for a moment to try to still the whirling in her head. Slowly, in painful increments, the gondola stopped its violent sideways motion and settled into a more even progress up the mountain. Ominous grinding noises drifted down from overhead.

They were now thirty feet up, she guessed.

When the dizziness subsided she opened her eyes to find Luca peering down toward the ground. He gave her a firm nod. "We're okay so far. If we stay still, it will be less stress to the cable."

No worries there. Ava's body was frozen, rigid with fear. She'd ridden the gondola countless times before without so much as a moment of discomfort. It's just like those times, she told herself. Riding up the mountain, looking forward to a day of fun, her mother's face pinked with cold, a rare smile gracing her lips.

Ava forced her muscles to relax, her fingers to unclench themselves from the edge of the seat.

We're going to be okay, she repeated to herself. The movement was gentle now, as they slid smoothly along the cable.

Sucking in a deep breath and letting it out, Ava felt her body begin to relax the tiniest bit. The gondola jerked to a halt so suddenly that she might have pitched right over the side if Luca hadn't gripped her jacket and anchored her down. Her scream echoed in the thin air.

The car swung in a crazy arc, all forward motion stopped.

They held on to each other and whatever they could reach, crouched on the floor as the hideous rocking continued, the blur of snow melting together with flashes of blue sky as they rocketed back and forth.

At any moment the gondola might detach, sending them crashing down.

Luca gripped her hand. She clung to him.

Cold air eddied around them, bringing tears to Ava's eyes.

Gradually, agonizingly, the movement slowed again until the gondola eased into stillness. No more moving in any direction, suspended in an eerie limbo. She could hear Luca's breath, coming in pants, along with her own. "What happened?" she whispered.

He looked up. "There's damage to the cable here. The gondola can't pass it."

She was too afraid to look down. "How high are we?"

"Probably forty feet."

The cable creaked and wind whistled past.

"Is it going to hold?" she managed. Her eyes told her the truth even if Luca could not. The cable above them trembled, one strand of metal wire springing loose from the bundle. There was no time to call for help. They were going to fall.

Another strand snapped and coiled away from the main cable sending shudders through the metal car.

Luca grabbed the rope from underneath the seat. He unwrapped it frantically mumbling to himself. "Maybe twenty feet, less the knot."

"What?" she said, eyes round with horror. "You are not saying what I think you are."

"We don't have a choice," he said, tying the rope around the window beam. "The rope will get you down twenty-plus feet and then you'll have to jump."

Her heart stopped. "I can't do that."

"Yes, you can and you're going to." He handed her a small penknife from his pocket. "If you can't get the knot undone, then cut yourself free from the rope. Get moving, this cable isn't going to hold much longer."

Before she knew it she had a rope tied around her waist and she was sitting at the open door, feet hanging over the side. Panic stormed through her. "I can't," she said.

He knelt next to her and talked in her ear, his strong body preventing her from backing up. His fingers stroked her hair and he pressed his mouth to her ear. "You can. I'm going to lower you down and when you get to the bottom you'll untie yourself and jump."

His voice was dead calm, as he they were discussing a trip to the beach.

"I…"

He brushed her hair aside and kissed her temple, sending tingles along her neck, then let his mouth trail along the hairline.

"You can do it, Ava. You were always the first one down the mountain, remember?"

"How will you get down?" she whispered, teeth chattering.

"I'll pull the rope up and do the same thing. Go," he said. "Go now."

She didn't know if she eased over the side or he maneuvered her, but she found herself hanging into space, spinning lazily on the rope. Her skin prickled in terror as the scenery swam in front of her eyes. She could hear Luca straining to brace himself against the side and let out the rope. She moved in bumps and jolts, each one making her want to scream in terror.

Even though she didn't dare look, she imagined Luca above her, looking down on her progress.

You can do it, Ava.

She tried to spread her arms and legs to slow the spinning. The ground whirled brilliantly beneath her as she descended.

When the last bump came, she heard Luca call. "You've got to jump now. Right now."

She couldn't move. The ground seemed an impossible distance away.

Groans came from the cable above, but her fingers still clutched tight to the rope. A round disk, a piece from the gondola's machinery broke loose and glanced off her shoulder as it dropped into the snow far below. She watched until it was swallowed up by the mantle of white.

She realized that Luca's life depended on her decision in that moment. The knot around her waist was cinched tight from her weight, so she pulled out the penknife, clutching it tight in her frozen fingers and began to saw furiously. It was slow going and the circling motion of her body dizzied her.

Soon her hand ached as the blade bit into the sturdy rope. Luca called out something which she could not decipher, but the intensity of his tone added new vigor to her efforts. Looping her arm around the rope above her she hacked away at the section tied around her waist.

One more small bit to go, and her nerves were screaming. Sawing frantically, she paid no heed to the raw spots forming on her skin. All at once the rope came loose, the breath pushed out of her as her body surged toward earth, held in place only by her arm as she dangled there.

She was not sure that she had the strength to let go and drop the twenty feet or so down to the ground.

What if she did not survive? What if she broke her back and became a paraplegic like her father?

Terror made her squeeze her eyes shut tight.

I can't do it.

I can't.

Another squeal from the cable sounded, louder.

If she did not drop, Luca would die.

She let loose her grip on the rope.

Luca saw her let go. He prayed he'd been right and the distance had not been enough to cripple or kill her. The gondola shuddered back and forth now, each movement eliciting eerie squeals from the gradually failing cable.

He hooked his arm around a pole to secure himself while he leaned over to coil the rope. Feverishly he reeled it in. It brought him back to their near escape from Melody Lake. He recalled the feel of Ava's limp body, the dead white of her face. His heart pounded and he knew it was not merely from the tension he now faced. In that moment, as in the present one, he was not helping Ava simply as a favor to her father or an excuse to do some treasure hunting. His actions were motivated by something richer, deeper and something he'd never felt so strongly before. The thought startled him but he reined himself in.

Priorities in order, Gage.

He noticed the knot securing the rope to the gondola had come almost loose. He unfastened it to retie the knot when another strand let go on the cable and the gondola lurched to the side. The rope fell from his hands and disappeared out the window of the gondola taking his only avenue of escape with it.

His breath puffed white in the air as he stared after the vanished rope. For a moment, he could not think, steeped in the impossible thought that there was no way out.

But he was not wired to accept defeat.

There was something here, some solution. He just had to find it.

On his knees now he examined the overhead cable again, the cut strands of steel beginning to curl.

He scanned quickly.

The drop here would surely kill him.

So the answer wasn't down there. His eyes traveled the length of the cable spanning the enormous distance between the shed and the final stop nearer the top of Whisper Mountain.

No way down…but maybe another way out.

It was crazy, too crazy to work. Victor had chided Luca endlessly over the years about his tendency to rush in first and worry about the consequences later.

Think it through, examine all the various possible outcomes, his brother would say.

Luca was the kid who would watch old black-and-white movies with his dad, admiring the swashbuckling daring and bravado of the many heroes who came to life there.

Sorry, Victor. It's time for some old-fashioned white-knuckle courage.

He stripped off his jacket, too amped to care about the stinging chill and carefully climbed on the still-bucking gondola seat. He lost his footing and went down to one knee, the car spiraling so rapidly he was dizzied.

He looked up for a moment, gaining equilibrium from the tranquil sky. When his vision steadied, he climbed out the window, hands clutched tightly to the freezing metal. It was like trying to stand on top of a moving train, so the best he could do was to stay low and grip with his feet and one hand, the other still clutching the jacket.

When he reached the roof of the gondola, he clung to the metal arm, extending his body along the length of it until he was close enough to reach.

He hoped.

Giving himself a mental countdown, he tossed one end of the jacket over the cable, while holding onto a sleeve. Somehow he manage to get the fabric up and over, until he could clasp both sleeves, tying them into as tight a knot as he was able.

He desperately hoped the nylon fabric would be enough, the cable would hold, the gondola would not careen down the cable and crush him at the bottom. Before he could ponder any more of the violent conclusions, he grabbed hold of his makeshift zip line and pushed off the gondola.

The jacket slid over the icy cable. Luca's body weight pulled frighteningly against the fabric, and he was sure it would rip in half, plummeting him down into the snow. It held, and he continued his downward progress back toward the shed. Every foot, every precious inch even, would bring him closer to the ground and farther away from the possibility that the fall would kill him.

The cable dipped as another strand let go. He was still a good thirty feet above the ground. His progress slowed to a stop as the jacket encountered friction probably caused by the deterioration of the cable.

He grabbed it, cutting his hands as he maneuvered his way over the rough patch until he was able to slide again, his progress slower now.

Thirty feet to the shed, he estimated.

Down below he saw something moving, dark against the snow.

Ava.

The breath whooshed out of him.

She'd not been hurt in her fall.

The knowledge gave him a surge of new energy as he worked his way across another rough patch on the cable.

In another fifteen feet he'd be through the worst of it.

His nerves relaxed just for a moment.

Until he heard the sound of tearing fabric.

NINETEEN

He was crazy. Or she was hallucinating. She wiped her eyes, but Luca was still there, sliding down the cable toward the shed, using his jacket as a harness. He'd stopped to wriggle past several sticking points along the wire and each time, her heart convulsed. The cable quivered violently now, the gondola shuddering, and Luca made tedious progress toward the shed.

She texted Stephanie, not really thinking there was much Luca's sister could do save what Ava was doing, standing, heart pounding, praying. Could Luca actually make it back to the shed with a flimsy improvised harness? Her emotions alternated between terror and exhilaration as he moved along the cable.

He stopped suddenly, and Ava's heart thumped. Legs flailing, Luca appeared to be fighting against some problem she could not identify. One of his hands came loose and he hung by one fist to the cable.

"Luca," she screamed.

He didn't answer, but his jacket fluttered down through the air in tatters.

Of course the wire had cut through it.

She looked upslope. The cable would not hold much longer, and Luca was still thirty feet or so in the air. In the distance she saw Stephanie appear over the top of the hill, Tate and Mack Dog at her heels. She stopped suddenly, and Ava knew that she saw immediately the danger her brother was in.

She took off toward them at a run, the heavy snow impeding her progress.

Ava turned again to Luca.

"It's going to break, Luca," she screamed.

He dropped down lower, now suspended from both hands and she almost screamed again. Then he began hand over hand to make his way down the cable toward the shed, as if he was a kid on the playground monkey bars.

He moved and she kept pace below as he closed the gap between them.

The blood roared loudly in her ears but not loud enough to drown out the horrendous snap of the cable giving way. The sound went through her like a gunshot as the gondola plummeted to the ground and Luca began to free fall.

Ava had heard people say that accidents sometimes unrolled in slow motion to the horrified observer. She now understood what they meant. Luca hung there motionless for a long moment until the recoil of the wire made him jerk like a helpless rag doll. He fell along with the cable until he was snapped free and flung to the ground, his body somersaulting over and over until he disappeared into the snow some distance away. Mercifully, he was tossed clear from the wreckage of the gondola car which was now imprisoned in a deep crater of snow.

She ran.

It was rough going in the freshly fallen snow and she repeatedly broke through the crust of snow before hauling herself up again. She saw no sign of Luca.

Stephanie caught up, panting. "Where is he?"

Tate was still a ways off, his weak leg slowing him down. Mack Dog, however, crossed the snow easily, leaping when the surface was too soft and scrambling through the troughs Stephanie had made in her approach.

The dog stiffened at some sound they could not hear and made his ungainly way over to the mountain of snow that had collected along the supports for the shed. Ava could see now that the snow was disturbed, plowed into a deep trough as if a mole had made its way through the thick blanket.

Stephanie and Ava flailed around in Mack Dog's wake, calling Luca's name.

They followed after the excited barking until Stephanie yelled out.

"Here. He's here."

She had a grip on the hem of his jeans. Ava could

see nothing else of Luca due to his shroud of snow. She felt around for his other ankle and they began to pull him out of the snowbank.

"Try not to twist his body," Stephanie said.

Ava didn't remind her she'd had enough ski patrol experience to know not to move a patient unnecessarily. They had no choice but to free him from the freezing shroud.

His body easily slid away from the burrow, and they were able to get him onto a relatively solid patch of snow. Stephanie feverishly brushed the icy piles away, and Ava knelt with trembling fingers to check for a pulse.

"Called for an ambulance," Tate said as he arrived. "They've got to get a plow through first. Chopper's out on another call."

Ava's fingers still sought the steady beat on Luca's throat. As far as she could see, there was no trauma to his head under which Tate was gingerly sliding his jacket to separate Luca's torso from the freezing ground.

Please, please, please.

She was afraid to believe there could be another outcome different than the terrible stillness that seemed to fall over her life when her mother died.

People died.

No, people were taken.

Violently.

Unexpectedly.

Tragically.

She'd learned the angry truth of that and tutored her heart in the lesson.

Yet, she still found herself straining to feel that precious beat, her spirit seized with some illogical hope that she could not explain. In that moment, she knew that if Luca was lost, her heart would be, too.

She pressed the pads of her fingers against his windpipe and traced them up to the hollow of his throat.

Stephanie was leaning over her now, her lips trembling.

And Ava felt a pulse.

"He's alive," she said, putting her cheek to his mouth to confirm he was still breathing.

Ava began checking his extremities for obvious injuries. He groaned when she touched his shoulder. She'd never been more thrilled at a sound before.

"Ambulance is stuck at the bottom of the mountain, waiting for a snowplow," Tate said, one hand over his phone. "They'll reroute the chopper as soon as they can."

Ava almost wailed aloud. "He can't wait. We've got to get him off the snow."

The revving of an engine made them all turn. A big bear of a man roared up on a snowmobile.

"Bully," Ava cried, "how did you get up here?"

He climbed off. "I was out for a spin. Thought I'd check in because I hadn't heard from you for a couple of days. Got here just in time to see the gondola come down. What were you doing on that death trap anyway?"

"Never mind that now," Stephanie said. "I saw a toboggan in the garage. You can take him down the road to meet the ambulance."

"Sure," Bully said. "Glad to help."

By the time Stephanie and Tate retrieved the toboggan, Sue and Goren arrived, panting. Ava filled them in.

"Is he badly hurt?" Sue asked, eyes huge.

"I don't know," Ava answered.

Goren shook his head. "I can't wait to get off this mountain."

They attached the toboggan to the snowmobile and loaded Luca aboard as carefully as possible. Stephanie climbed on behind Bully. "Meet me at the hospital as soon as you can," she said before they took off.

Ava did not think of it until a moment later.

The snowmobile tracks that she and Luca had seen earlier before they'd ascended to the shed. Bully said he had arrived only just in time to see Luca fall, but maybe he was lying.

Luca opened his eyes to see a blurry face staring at him. At first he thought he was dreaming, but the face steadied and drew clearer.

Ava peered at him, Stephanie and Tate pressed in close behind her. He jerked causing them all to jump, wincing as a lancing pain cut through his shoulder.

Ava smiled widely.

"What are you grinning for?" he demanded. "My shoulder is killing me."

"Because, aside from a concussion and a dislocated shoulder which the doctor fixed," Stephanie cut in, "you are perfectly fine."

He blinked as the memory came back. The cable failing. His spectacular plummet to earth after his jacket ripped to shreds. "Of course I'm fine. I had an excellent escape plan."

Ava laughed loud and long. He would have taken offense if he hadn't enjoyed the sound so much.

"How did I get here?"

Ava explained about Bully. Her furrowed brow made him further question her.

"I'm going to go to the trailer park and talk to him," she said. "To find out what he was really doing there."

Luca nodded and edged to the side of the bed. "I'll go, too."

"Oh, no," Ava and Stephanie said in unison.

"You're not going anywhere until tomorrow morning," Stephanie finished. "Doctor's orders."

He eyed both women. "There is no way I'm staying overnight." So maybe his head was pounding like someone was beating his skull with a mallet, but he was not going to be imprisoned in a hospital.

Stephanie put a hand on his chest. "You can't leave until the doctor releases you," she repeated.

"That's not how it works. This is a hospital, not a jail." He tried to scoot off the bed again.

Stephanie folded her arms across her chest. "It is if you're in restraints. They do that if they think you might be a danger to yourself, you know, pending a psychological workup."

He stared. "And who exactly is going to put me in restraints?"

She eyed him placidly. "Dad donated the money for the trauma unit. One phone call and I'm sure I could have you held here for an evaluation. You are just crazy enough to do yourself bodily harm."

"You wouldn't do that," he rasped.

"Don't try me." Stephanie settled gracefully in the chair. "We're both staying here until you get a clean bill of health. There are still a few more tests that haven't come back."

Luca shot an exasperated look at Tate. "Are you going to let your wife get away with this?"

Tate shrugged. "She doesn't need my permission to keep you from doing something dumb."

Luca fumed, his mood made even fouler by the sparking pain in his shoulder. "This is unbelievable."

Even though he protested loudly and vigorously to everyone within earshot, it did no good. The best he could do was make Ava promise not to go speak to Bully until he was released.

"The police are waiting to talk to me and then I have to go finalize arrangements for my uncle's memorial service anyway," she said, a wave of sadness passing across her face that momentarily derailed his ire.

She came to the edge of the bed and pressed a kiss to his forehead, her lips soft and gentle. He could not stop himself from tipping his face up, his mouth in search of hers, but she had moved away.

"That was the craziest thing I've ever seen, and I'm glad you're okay," she said before she left.

Then she was gone.

For a second, his heart felt light, dancing above the pain that rolled through his body.

Sergeant Towers came in, expression unruffled as ever, listening attentively as Luca gave his account. "So you figure the person who pushed you was Sue, Harold or Goren?"

"Or Bully," Luca added.

Towers did not seem surprised by the addition to the list. "I've known Sue and Harold a long time. Bully, too."

"And you think they wouldn't have done such a thing."

His mouth quirked at the corner. "I've learned in this job that even normal, average people can do the unthinkable if they believe they have a good reason." He paused. "Passions can run high."

Stephanie stood. "What kind of passions?"

"The usual. Money, power, love."

"Was Sue still in love with Paul?"

The officer frowned. "Not Paul."

Luca heard the slight hesitation in his voice. "Who, then?"

Towers zipped his jacket. "If you want to know all the dirt, you'll have to rake it up yourself. I'm not a gossip columnist. Have a nice afternoon." The door closed softly behind him.

Luca shifted, causing his shoulder to throb. "What do you make of that?"

"I don't know, but maybe we better take a closer look at Sue Agnoti," she said. "For now," Stephanie said, opening the laptop Tate brought from the lodge after the plow cleared the road, "because we're going to be here a while, we might as well solve this treasure mystery, don't you think?"

As much as he wanted to turn his back on his infuriating sister, he tried to put it behind him. "What do you hear from Victor?"

"Glad you asked," she said. "He said to tell you that he's always suspected you're certifiably insane."

"Yeah, yeah," Luca grumped. "What about the printing press business?"

"Victor is a wealth of information, as he promised. He credits the invention of the first real successful press to the German Johannes Gutenberg around 1440. The man was actually a goldsmith, ironically, and he created an alloy of lead, tin and antimony that was durable enough to be used in the press. The separate pieces of type could be re-used and rearranged."

Luca wished his head would stop pounding long enough for him to think it through. "Maybe Paul got hold of a part of the press, some of the original movable type. It would be worth a fortune. That would explain the size of the box and the book about printing presses."

"I'll do a search and see if I can figure out what something like that would cost."

"Could be he got his hands on an old book, one of Gutenberg's early efforts."

"I thought we were looking for the Sunset Star," Tate put in. "What does this all have to do with a pearl?"

Luca closed his eyes and pictured the verse from Matthew and half mumbled to himself, "One pearl of great price." He looked up to find Tate and Stephanie staring at him. "Maybe Paul found that pearl."

"Only it isn't a pearl at all," Stephanie finished.

"And someone else is after it." Luca thought of Ava. She would not be safe until they found the treasure.

And he had to make sure they found it before Paul's killer did.

TWENTY

Ava felt a twinge of guilt after bumming a ride off a local and heading to Peak Season late that afternoon. She'd promised Luca, but she could not keep her word. Her heart still echoed with the terror of seeing him hanging on the cable, awakening feelings she could not tolerate. The twin urges to both run from Whisper Mountain and the ludicrous hope that she might find a treasure that would save her family home warred inside her, too.

She could make sense of none of it except the knowledge that she needed to immediately put an end to the spiraling chaos, before anyone else got hurt.

Her fingers curled into tight fists at the memory of frantically searching for a pulse on Luca's cold, still body. She would not allow anyone else to die on Whisper Mountain, especially Luca.

Pushing away all disturbing thoughts, she crunched up the walkway.

It was stupid to come and talk to Bully alone,

but deep down in her heart, she believed he had not harmed Paul. Not Bully, the man who used to pull her on a sled when she'd visited Uncle Paul and helped her make a massive snow monster that put the other kids' sculptures to shame.

Hand raised to knock, she felt someone grip her shoulder.

She whirled to find herself staring at the angry face of Luca Gage.

His face was lined with pain and his right arm swathed in a sling. "You promised me you wouldn't come here alone."

She caught her breath. "You look terrible. What are you doing out of the hospital?"

"Tests came back fine, and Stephanie couldn't go through with her threat to have me tied up like a rabid dog, so I discharged myself."

"That wasn't smart."

"Neither is this," he said, jerking a thumb at the door. "Someone is trying to kill you or me or both of us and you just walk right up here like a lamb to the slaughter. How does that make sense exactly? Explain it to me."

"This is my problem. I don't want you risking your life again."

"It's mine to risk, and what about you? You've got a father who loves you and I…"

"And?"

He huffed. "And I think this whole plan to confront Bully alone is ridiculous. Besides, you broke your promise."

She could not resist a smile at his petulant tone, like a boy whose buddy had chosen someone else for the kickball team. "I'm sorry I broke my promise, but I stand by the decision. Let me handle it alone."

He straightened, although the effort made him wince. "And what if I refuse to do that?"

She opened her mouth to retort when the door suddenly opened and Bully stood in his usual jeans and flannel shirt, chewing on a toothpick.

"If you two lovebirds are gonna raise a ruckus, maybe you should do it somewhere else."

Luca's cheeks pinked and Ava felt her own cheeks flush. "We're not… Never mind. I need to talk to you, Bully."

His eyes narrowed a fraction. "Cops already came an hour ago, asked me what I was doing up the mountain. I told them same thing I told you."

"You were there before the cable snapped. We saw the tracks," Luca said.

"You're mistaken," Bully said. "All this treasure hunting is making you paranoid." He started to close the door, but Ava held it open as a piece of the puzzle snapped into place.

"Hang on. I finally remembered what's been bugging me. That night when someone yanked me under the trailer. We told you about the box and you said Paul probably only found fake jewelry. You specifically mentioned a cameo."

"So?"

Luca fisted his good hand on his hip. "We found a stash of jewelry at the lodge and it had a cameo in it."

Bully went still. "Cameos are pretty common. My mother had one and her sister did also. Don't prove anything."

Ava pulled the other detail into place. "Your vest, the down one you always wear. I noticed it had a tear in the fabric on the back." She locked eyes with him. "You got it crawling under Paul's trailer, didn't you? You knew there was a cameo in that box because you opened it."

Bully looked from Luca to Ava, considering. "Yeah, I opened it. So what? Paul owed me a nice chunk of change for rent, and I knew he was gonna skip town again before I ever saw a dime of it. I noticed he was fussing around with something under the trailer couple days before his accident. I crawled under there while he was gone and took a look. Not easy. I got stuck for a while."

Ava felt like her heart would beat out of her rib cage. "What was in it, Bully? What was in the box?"

"Some jewelry, on top of something all wrapped up. I couldn't get a good look at it 'cause there wasn't enough space to open the box all the way." He looked down. "I was going to go back later and take it out, but he must have moved it because when I looked inside again, the contents were gone. Next day, so was Pauly."

Ava's throat thickened. "Oh, Bully, I wish you had told us before."

His gaze was riveted to the ground. "I was just looking out for myself. I never hurt your uncle. Never laid a hand on him."

"Why should we believe that? You still haven't given us a good reason for being on Whisper Mountain this morning," Luca said.

Bully's head came up and he folded his arms. "That's like I told you. Just checking in."

"I don't believe that," Luca said.

His mouth tightened. "You believe what you want, sonny, but I don't think you're in a position to judge me." The challenge in his eyes was clear.

"Why is that?" Luca retorted.

"You're not from around here. You're some rich kid who came to spend the winters and then leave to go back to your fancy house and fancy cars. And why are you here now? Not to fix Ava's problems or help lay her uncle to rest. You're here to find the treasure, or maybe you're interested in buying up Whisper."

Luca stiffened. "You don't know what you're talking about."

"Don't I? Your rich daddy owns a share in Gold Summit, don't he? Would be a pretty neat deal to tack on Whisper. Sticking around until you convince Ava to sell it to you?"

Luca's eyes went wild with anger.

Ava stepped between them.

"Bully, I'm sorry," she said. "Of course I know you didn't hurt Uncle Paul. I want you to come to the memorial tomorrow morning at Whisper."

Bully was still staring at Luca. "Sure you want me to come? Seems I'm under a cloud of suspicion."

"Paul would want you there. Please. Ten o'clock."

Bully shrugged. "I'll check my calendar." He bobbed his chin at Ava. "Be careful, honey. You're getting confused about who your friends are."

He closed the door.

Luca stalked down the steps, stopping so suddenly that she almost plowed into him from behind. He whirled to face her.

"That's not true what he said. I'm not here to take your treasure or pressure you to sell. Do you believe that?"

His green eyes gleamed in the rich winter sun.

Did she believe that? When he had so much to gain? Looking into his battered face she felt a flutter deep inside, a curl of warmth that started at her toes and worked its way up to her throat. "Yes, I do."

He sighed and reached an arm around to pull her close. Her heart sped up at the strong embrace, the warmth of his chin on her head. "I would never hurt you," he whispered.

She wanted nothing more than to stay in that embrace, to hold tight to the comfort he offered, but Bully was partially correct. Luca would go when the treasure was found, back to his life, his future, which would happen far away from Whisper Mountain.

You're right, Luca, she thought, pain trickling through the pleasure. *You won't hurt me, because I won't let you.* She allowed herself one more moment of tenderness before she pulled out of his arms.

They waited for Stephanie to pick them up. Luca remained silent on the trip back up to the lodge. His body protested at each bump and turn, and he was still irritated that Ava was bent on pursuing the investigation on her own. Their time together was coming to a close. All he could do was figure out who was after the treasure, if indeed there was actually a treasure to be found at all.

The wall had fallen back into place, the connection he'd felt between them severed. Maybe deep down she really did still question his motives. He was beginning to question them himself. Why was he taking her withdrawal so personally?

He had the sinking feeling she'd been building walls around herself since the moment her mother drowned in Melody Lake. Nothing he did or didn't do would change that. Only God had the power, and even He couldn't change a heart that didn't want to be altered.

Luca noted Charlie Goren's car was gone when they arrived as the sun mellowed into a pastel sunset. Sue was already deep in preparations for the memorial, and Ava dived in, helping prepare sandwiches and potato salad, enough for dozens of guests, although Ava did not expect any visitors at all.

They would be lucky to round up a half dozen people bent on showing their respects but Luca kept that comment to himself. Everyone worked hard to keep him idle. He was not allowed to move a single table or even wipe down the counter. Aggravated to no end, he was relieved when everyone grabbed quick sandwiches and excused themselves to go to bed.

"I'm staying in Uncle Paul's room," Ava told him firmly.

He didn't have time to muster a reply before she continued. "I've made up my mind."

"I'm selling the resort to the highest bidder right after the memorial. If that's your dad, he's welcome to it."

"There's still a chance we can find the treasure."

"It's not worth the risk. I'm selling Whisper."

A small cry came from the hallway. Sue came in, arms wrapped around herself. "No, Ava, don't do that. Your father needs more time to heal, then he'll come back and things will turn around."

Ava showed surprised at Sue's naïveté. "My dad isn't going to walk again. He's accepted that."

"We can help him. Put in more ramps." Her eyes glittered. "Have his car outfitted with hand controls."

"No, Sue. He's behind my decision to sell."

"But, but I thought…" her mouth went slack.

"What did you think?" Luca asked gently. Towers's strange comment flashed through his memory.

Was Sue in love with Paul?

Not Paul.

He exchanged a look with Ava and he saw his own confusion mirrored on her face. "Sue," Ava said, taking her hand. "Why is it so important to you that my father come back?"

Sue clenched Ava's fingers. "I just wanted it to be all right again, like it was before."

"It can't be that way, not after my mother killed herself."

"Maybe she didn't," Sue said, yanking her hands away. "Maybe it was an accident and she fell in."

"Why do you say that?"

"I've just had a lot of time to think over the years. This place doesn't have to be a place of sadness, honey. It can be a new start."

"It's not going to happen. You've done a great job trying to keep Whisper in one piece. I'm grateful, and so is my father." Ava moved closer as if to embrace Sue, but she kept out of reach.

Sue's voice was low, intense. "Your father has nothing to thank me for."

She walked stiffly away.

Ava puzzled over Sue's odd reaction as she pulled on a pair of sweats and a T-shirt and got between the cold sheets. Mack Dog seemed disgruntled to be keeping Ava company instead of his newly adopted master, Tate, but Luca insisted. Sue had to know selling was the only option. What bothered her more was Sue's suggestion that her mother's death was an accident.

Ava's mind drifted back to that horrible night. Her mother and father had been fighting. She'd heard their voices loud, though muffled, through the bedroom walls. Her adult mind found it perfectly understandable.

A man dealing with his sudden crippling.

A woman with a history of depression struggling over near bankruptcy and her husband's frail condition.

Fights were natural and this one had seemed no worse than the others.

Then the squeak of her father's wheelchair as he banged away down the hallway, past her door. Later, a quiet descended on the house until she heard the door open and saw, through the tiny upstairs window, her mother walking along the path into a delicate curtain of falling snow.

Ava's body tensed, as it always did when she allowed her mind to travel back in time. Why hadn't she run after her mother? Pressed herself into that dark cloud of sadness until she forced a smile out of Marcia Stanton. Would one smile have been enough to change her terrible decision that day?

Tears coursed down Ava's face.

Why, Mom?

Why, God?

She had not asked Him in a very long time. It was like she'd told Luca.

I can't pray. I can't pray anymore.

Then I'll pray for both of us.

She'd never imagined that someone else would hold her up to God. Would God reject her? she wondered. Cast His eyes away from her rage and bitterness?

He knows how hard that is for us sometimes.

God knew. Then why didn't He send comfort?

She thought about Luca who was praying for her.

Why, God?

There was still no answer, just the same silence as before, but she felt a sense of something different. Something that felt strangely like comfort.

TWENTY-ONE

The pitiful collection of guests began to arrive. Ava saw their cars pull up, one by one. Charlie Goren, Bully, a couple from town who knew Uncle Paul only casually as far as she could ascertain. When she forced herself to join the others, she found Sue dressed in black pants and a soft sweater tidying up the kitchen. Harold had exchanged his worn jeans for a less-worn pair of khakis and a polo shirt. Stephanie, Luca and Tate showed up looking somber. Mack Dog was relegated to outside.

Sue had managed to convince the local pastor to come and say a few words. He kept it generic. No one had many good things to say about her uncle. It was over in a painfully short time before the guests were sent to partake of the food.

Charlie Goren bobbed his head at Ava. "I'm sorry about your loss. And I'm sorry you never found the Sunset Star. Luca told me it was most likely sold."

She nodded. "I wish we'd had a better ending. I know how much you wanted to see the Sunset Star."

Goren offered a smile. "I did, but no one would have appreciated a treasure like that more than Paul."

True enough, and the memory of his endless enthusiasm brightened her spirits momentarily. She thanked Goren with a heartfelt squeeze to his hand and accepted condolences from Bully who looked unhappy to be there in a button-up shirt and boots. "You know how I feel. Anything you need, just tell old Bully."

Luca began to head her way. Her heart sped up and she looked desperately around for a place to avoid him and the mixed-up feelings he stirred in her. Her cell phone rang. Her father's number popped up, and she quickly returned to Uncle Paul's room to answer it.

"Avy, am I interrupting the service?"

"No, Dad."

"I just wanted to say I'm sorry."

"Me, too. I was unkind when we spoke earlier." She swallowed hard. "I know you had your reasons for distrusting Uncle Paul."

"Thanks for saying that. I sure wish I could be there with you."

"I wish you could, too. Sue and Harold worked so hard to spruce the place up." She asked him about his health, reassuring herself that the doctors pronounced his recovery on track.

"Dad, Sue said something odd." She told him about the conversation, expecting him to be as bewildered as she. Instead she was met by a silence that went on far too long. "Dad?"

He cleared his throat. "This isn't the time to talk about it. Not over the phone."

A strange feeling of dread coalesced in her stomach. "You have to tell me."

Another extended pause. "That day, the day your mother died. There was some unpleasantness."

"What kind?"

"I didn't want you to ever hear this, Ava."

"Hear what? If you don't tell me, I'll have to ask Sue. Please, Dad."

He sucked in a breath. "Your mother accused me of loving another woman."

Ava's mouth fell open. "Sue?"

"Yes." He huffed. "I should be there telling you in person. Sue became attached to me, even more so after my accident. I kept her at arm's length, but she insisted on telling me that day that she loved me. Your mom overheard and went ballistic."

Ava forced out the words. "Dad, did you love Sue?"

"No, honey. As a matter of fact, I wanted her to leave months earlier, when I began to get the idea she had feelings for me, but your mother was so fond of her, and I thought it would exacerbate her problems to be alone on Whisper Mountain without another woman around. Stupid call on my part."

"So that night, Mom accused you and later…"

"She drowned."

She heard the grief in those two hard syllables. "Sue said it might not have been an accident. Maybe she slipped."

He cleared his throat. "I've thought about it, obsessed really, for years over that very thing. I think that version is easier on her conscience. She doesn't want to believe she contributed to your mother's decision."

"But you think Mom killed herself."

"The police thought so."

She gripped the phone so hard her hand ached. "Tell me what you believe."

"Your mother was suicidal at several points over the course of our marriage, but…"

Ava leaned forward.

"The very last moment of her life was between her and God. I've always told you that we don't know what happened in those last few seconds."

Those last few seconds. Had she walked in willingly? Fallen in accidentally?

The final moment of her life was between her and God. But, oh, the heartache that moment left behind for Ava and her father.

"You didn't tell me about Sue. All these years."

His tone hardened. "No. I took that guilt on all by myself, Ava. I should have fired Sue months before. I should have gone after Marcia. God forgive me, I should have done so many things differently, but I didn't."

Ava was fighting back tears. "Sue was hoping all this time that you'd come back to Whisper Mountain."

His voice was so soft. "She never could see the truth. My heart always belonged to Marcia. There was no room for anyone else, except you."

"Oh, Dad. Part of me hates this place."

"I feel the same way, Ava, but the other part of me knows Whisper Mountain holds all the greatest treasures of my life."

Ava mumbled incoherently for a while, letting her father's soothing words wash over her, their grief binding them together. She said goodbye when someone knocked softly on the door.

She opened it to find Luca and Stephanie there. Luca shoved his good hand in his pocket. "We, uh, we came to check on you." He eyed her tearstained face. "We can come back later."

"No," she said. "Come in. I need the company." Even though she wanted to keep her father's revelation to herself, she found it all coming out in spurts as Stephanie and Luca looked on in astonishment.

Stephanie shook her head. "I never would have guessed that about Sue."

"Me, neither, but it makes sense." He glanced out the window at Tate who was roughhousing with Mack Dog. "I wonder…"

"If Sue had something to do with Paul's death?"

"Securing the treasure would ensure Whisper wouldn't be sold. She'd still have a chance of getting Bruce to come back."

"But there is no treasure," Ava groaned. "No reason for anyone to kidnap Paul."

Luca cocked his head. "I've been thinking about that printing press."

Stephanie shot a look at Ava. "Between Luca and Victor I've gotten chapter and verse on Gutenberg and his printing press. He started printing the Bible. The number of lines per page was increased from forty to forty-two to save paper, so those Bibles were given the name B42s. Print runs were increased to a whopping 180 copies. Pope Pius XI even gave his work a thumbs-up. I could go on and on."

"Maybe Paul got hold of a Gutenberg book. The size of the box under the trailer indicates something big," Luca said, chuckling as he watched Mack Dog knock Tate over backward into the snow and dive on top of him.

"Unlikely," Stephanie said. "There are fewer than two dozen in the whole world and a complete copy hasn't been sold since 1978. If he was really lucky, he might have found pieces, a page or two."

"Uncle Paul never had that kind of luck." Ava remembered her uncle's last words.

This time I'm going to make it right.

What could he have found that gave him such confidence? It didn't matter anymore. Whatever

it was could stay buried in some dark hole somewhere, along with Sue's futile love for her father,
her mother's tortured last moments and all the
happy times when things had been good.

Luca's boyish face rose in her heart, his brash
laughter as he'd flown down the snow-covered
mountain behind her. Maybe Whisper would belong to the Gages. Maybe Luca would enjoy the
slopes again, at some other time, with some other
girl. The thought cut a painful path through her
insides.

"I should get back to the guests," she said. "The
real estate agent is coming later this afternoon to
talk over the details."

"We'll be packed up and out of here after the service," Luca said, eyes riveted to her face. "If that's
what you want."

She did not dare meet his gaze. Luca belonged
to another world; she'd been wrong to let him into
her heart and mind.

Cut the threads to Whisper. Cut them all.

"I think that would be best," she managed before
escaping into the hallway.

Luca packed silently. Stephanie and Tate did the
same, loading everything into Stephanie's car. Tate
took Mack Dog out for one more play session, and
Luca and his sister watched, leaning against the
car in the brilliant sunshine beaming down from a

cloudless sky. The mountain was bathed in white, a perfect backdrop for the quaint old lodge.

"Will Dad buy it?" Stephanie asked.

"I don't know." At first he'd wanted desperately to insist on it, but now he realized, without Ava, Whisper Mountain was just another ski resort, one of many strung along the Sierras. Without Ava...

The words replayed over and over.

What would she do? Pay off her debts and move on to a new life, close to her father probably. Would she find happiness?

He prayed she would, but still, the heaviness in his own heart did not let up, intensifying when Ava stepped out of the lodge and headed toward him.

"I'm going to go see if I can tear Tate away from Mack Dog." Stephanie crunched away, waving at Ava as she passed.

Luca's pulse ticked up a notch as Ava drew close, hair a luminous glow against the winter panorama.

She gave him a nod. "All packed?"

"Yes. Tate is just saying his goodbyes to Mack Dog."

Ava sighed. "Do you think he'd want to take Mack?"

Luca blinked. "I think he'd be thrilled, but are you okay with that?"

Ava shook her head. "I'll miss him, but it seems like it's the right thing to do. Leave it all behind and start over."

Luca didn't think. He reached out and took her hands. "There's no other choice?"

She inhaled, her breath shaky. "No, there's too much baggage here." Her voice dropped. "Too much baggage in me."

He can lift that away, Luca wanted to say. There is love waiting for you here if you'll just open your eyes. "Ava…"

They were interrupted as Tate and Stephanie ran toward them, Tate holding something in his hands.

"What do you make of this?" he said, holding out Mack Dog's collar. "It came off when we were wrestling."

They bent close together to look. Luca could make out some scratches on the metal tag. He peered closer. "It says B42."

Ava's mouth fell open. "Like the B42 Bible?"

"Maybe," he said. "Or maybe it's a hint to tell us where he's hidden this treasure."

"Or both," Stephanie said, eyes sparking in excitement. "I'm thinking about those old lockers. Is there a locker number B42?"

Ava nodded. "Yes, there is."

Luca moved closer, praying that this wasn't just another dead end to keep Ava from leaving her pain in the past. "Are you up for one more shot at this treasure hunting business?"

Ava smiled, that open-mouthed, joyful grin that set his nerves on fire. "What could it hurt?" she said.

* * *

They brainstormed on the way, heading to the garage for a set of sturdy bolt cutters.

Mack Dog broke from the group and approached an old relic of a truck, climbing nimbly into the back and curling up there.

Tate laughed. "Never misses an opportunity for a nap."

"I guess you'll have to take the truck with you when you go. It's his favorite spot," Ava teased.

Tate's face flushed. "You…want me to take him?"

She nodded, her heart filling with warmth. "He loves you, and that's what Uncle Paul would want, too."

Tate only nodded, but Ava could see he was thrilled to the core. She had made one right decision at least.

Stephanie spoke excitedly as they headed outside, her words keeping pace with their vigorous hike. "John Danson's great-grandfather worked at the Leuven library," she said excitedly. "It was burned in World War II. Guess what book was the star of their collection and presumably lost in the fire according to the text I just got from big brother?"

Ava's heart thudded. "A Gutenberg Bible?"

"Right on the money."

"Okay," Luca said, leading them past the main lodge and along a path Harold had recently cleared.

"So maybe Great-Grandfather Danson takes the Bible before the library was burned. He doesn't want to admit to the theft, so he keeps it quiet, hides it away."

"And when they come to the States, he can't sell it without people putting the pieces together and realizing he stole it from the library."

"So it's put away in storage, along with some costume jewelry and musty old books."

"He goes to the grave carrying his secret with him. The book is lost until Uncle Paul borrows money from Charlie Goren and buys the storage unit, thinking he might find the pearl."

"And he did," Luca said. "This time maybe Paul really did find it. It just didn't look like what he thought it would."

They found the locker quickly. Number B42 was in good condition, sandwiched as it was in the middle of long rows of lockers. The building that housed the lockers was sound, no leaking from the roof. Aside from a few dented locker doors and the smell of long years of disuse, the place was in good shape.

Luca bent down and peered at the lock on B42. "This is the one."

He handed her the bolt cutters. "Do you want to do the honors?"

Cheeks warm, she took it from his hand and applied herself to cutting through the hanging padlock. The metal gave way with a click and she tossed the lock aside. With fingers gone cold, she tried the locker door. It refused to budge until she gave it a hard yank and the panel pulled open with a squeal of protest.

She was frozen for a moment. If there was nothing inside, then it truly was the end. For Paul's dream. And for hers. She took a deep breath and looked inside.

TWENTY-TWO

Luca realized he was holding his breath as Ava reached in the locker and pulled out a compact bundle wrapped in oilcloth.

Luca frowned. "Strange size. It should be…"

A shadow slid across the floor toward them as a man stepped around the corner holding a shotgun.

Charlie Goren stood, shifting back and forth like a runner at the starting line, gripping and regripping the weapon. "Whatever that is, it's mine."

Ava appeared too shocked to reply.

Luca edged in front of her and Tate did the same for Stephanie. "How exactly is it yours?" Luca asked, voice level.

"Because Paul borrowed money from me to buy it. I thought it would be a pearl, but at this point, I'll take what I can get."

"Did you kidnap my uncle?" Ava said.

Goren twitched. "He boasted and boasted all the years I knew him. Behind every boast was a dig, I'm smarter than you, I'm luckier, I'm better. I let it go until he came back the last time. It was the big score, he said. I did some research on the Dansons and for once, it seemed like he had the facts to back him up." Goren spat the words. "I knew he was lying about what he got. I made up my mind to grab Paul and make him tell me what he'd found in that storage box."

"You're responsible for his death," Ava said flatly.

Goren shifted. "Things went wrong. He hid the treasure up here before I could get it from under his trailer. Then he arranged a meeting with you. I had to stop that before he handed it over. I was going to let him go after he cooperated, but we crashed and he didn't survive. I had no choice but to get out of there."

Ava hugged herself. "He trusted you."

"No, he didn't. He didn't trust anyone. Every time he pursued another payoff, he kept the particulars to himself. All he needed from me was my money and I guess he was really the smarter one because I gave it to him. Handed it over as if he was my own brother."

"It doesn't give you the right to do what you did."

Goren looked at her, wide-eyed. "For once, I decided to be the one in charge. Just once. I knew he hid things under his trailer. I tried to sneak under and hopefully find the pearl, but I got you instead. Stupid, stupid. I should have known it was here somewhere, here at Whisper. I slashed my own tires so I'd have a reason to stick around." He laughed, a half-hysterical sound. "I broke the basement window and all I got for my trouble was an old book."

Ava felt anger brewing inside her. "How did you know Paul arranged the meeting with me?"

Goren stepped closer, his fingers tight around the gun. "I tried to dissuade you from searching here by sending those logs down on you, but here you are, so we'll do it the hard way. I want what was in the locker. It's mine."

Luca spoke calmly. "You're not a killer, Charlie. You're just a guy who got cheated."

Goren swallowed. "My store is all I have. My gems. I'll take them and start over with whatever treasure I can lay my hands on."

"Sure," Luca said. "But you don't need to kill anyone to do that."

"Not if she gives it to me." Goren poked the shotgun at Ava. "This time it's loaded and I'm going to be blamed for Paul's death. I've got nothing to lose."

Ava offered up the bundle. "Whatever is in here," she said, "I'd give it all to have my uncle back."

Goren didn't meet her eyes. He reached out and grabbed it with one hand. "Now all of you face the lockers and put your hands over your heads. Right now. I'm going to walk out that door and if anyone turns around I'm going to start shooting. I'm not a good marksman, but I'm sure I can get most of you."

They all turned around. Luca put his palms on the cold metal and tried to get a glimpse of Ava.

All the grief, all the pain could have been avoided if Paul had seen the real treasure right before his eyes, a niece who loved him in spite of his faults.

"Charlie, you don't have to do this," Luca said.

His words were cut short by a shot that nearly deafened him. Luca pulled Ava to the floor, heard Stephanie's scream echo through the small space. He saw Goren on the ground and the door to the locker building banging shut.

They scrambled to their feet. Goren was on his back, blood leaking from a bullet wound to his shoulder. The bundle was gone.

Goren groaned. "I'm a fool."

"Who shot you?" Luca barked.

"A fool," Goren continued, tears streaming down his face now.

Luca leaped to his feet and took off for the door.

"No," Stephanie hollered. "Luca, don't."

"Stay here with Goren," Luca shouted over his shoulder. "Call for help."

Then he crashed out the door, Ava right behind him.

There was no sign of the shooter, but the tracks in the snow made it clear that whoever it was had taken off around the side of the lodge. Most of the guests' cars were gone except for Bully's snowmobile and Goren's vehicle. Luca threw off the sling and increased his speed as much as he could, ignoring his protesting muscles.

He finally caught a glimpse of his quarry, wearing a ski cap and black pants, sprinting with surprising speed for the snowmobile. The facts lined themselves up. Luca would not catch up. It was not possible in his battered condition, but he continued the frantic pace anyway.

Just as he'd feared, the person hopped on the snowmobile and revved the engine, taking off on the thick blanket of snow and heading away from the road.

He stopped, gasping for breath. Ava pulled up next to him.

"Who…" She panted.

"I don't know."

Ava turned around and raced back to the lodge. To call the police, probably.

Luca kicked at a clump of snow. It couldn't end this way. No treasure. Goren's shooter free. Where was the closure for Ava? The happy ending? She deserved answers.

Suddenly Ava was back, thrusting a pair of skis at him and tossing a set of poles and boots at his feet.

She bent to yank on boots and stepped expertly into the skis, the bindings clicking into place.

"Dangerous," Luca growled.

"Then stay here and wait for the police. I'll tell you how it turns out."

She knew perfectly well he was not about to let her go after an armed shooter on her own, but she probably thought he wouldn't be able to keep up with an injured shoulder.

That's where you're wrong, Ava, he thought as he snapped on his own set of skis.

Ava poled hard as they trekked across the snow next to the road. It was irregular and marred from the snowplow, but soon the surface was smoother and they moved along, following the tracks of the snowmobile.

"There," Ava shouted, pointing at the rolling hill that fell away to their right.

"Slopes haven't been tended to," Luca called back.

He needn't have told her. She knew the terrain was dangerous here, without her father's constant vigilance. Above them was a cornice of snow, a massive thrust of white that had been hollowed at the base by wind and sun.

The snowmobile was speeding across the slope below that glittering cornice. On the other side lay an easy path down toward the main road. Luca was right. The scenario was a recipe for disaster. She should let their quarry go.

She thought of Paul and his infectious smile. It seemed like a lifetime ago she'd watched him snatched from right before her eyes by Goren. But Goren had not acted alone. Someone told him about Uncle Paul's plan to meet her. The same person who had gunned down Goren.

Their escape meant she would never really know.

Like she would never really know if her mother committed suicide or accidentally fell into that lake.

Maybe it didn't matter. They were both irretrievably lost to her.

But not completely. Something had happened to her in the time she'd been searching for this treasure. She realized in that moment that their lives would always be intertwined with hers, the good memories and the love lingering on more vibrant than the circumstances of their death.

Treasures.

From God.

Her heart swelled. Her treasures were secure. She would let the snowmobile go.

Luca moved closer and put an arm around her. She also knew the truth about him as clearly as if she'd realized it years ago. Turning, she caught the iridescent green eyes that seemed to look into the deepest part of her.

"I…" Her words were lost in a loud rush of sound as part of the cornice gave way. A corner of the ice mound broke off and slid down the slope, a few yards in front of the snowmobiler who stopped abruptly.

In one swift movement, the driver jerked the machine around and headed back toward Luca and Ava's position. Whether it was the movement of the snowmobile or the simple act of forces working on the unstable pile of snow, the mountainside began to tremble, signaling the onset of an avalanche.

In unison, Ava and Luca pointed their skis toward the grove of trees away from the steep slope. Poling hard, they leaned into the slope and shoved off. Cold wind slapped Ava's face and the roar of the monster river of snow followed them.

The snowmobile plowed ahead of them, kicking icy bits in its wake.

The ground shook under their skis. Ava risked a look back. A plume of snow roiled into the air. The white wave was almost upon them.

Luca shouted something that Ava couldn't make out. It seemed as though they were flying, like birds about to be enveloped by a white cloud. It was a beautiful image, but the reality was deadly.

Luca kept pace with her in spite of his bruises.

He'd risked everything, including his life to help her.

She knew she'd give it all up—the treasure, Whisper, even the chance to avenge her uncle's death—if it would protect him.

She didn't have time to ponder the strange and wondrous feeling as cascading snow rushed around her threatening to knock her over. Skiing for the farthest tree, she prayed the stout trunk would shield them from the onslaught. Instead she fell, her skis snapping off, her body crashing into the massive pine. Then Luca was there, his arms around her as the enormous strength of the avalanche pinned them together against the frozen bark.

Her cheek pressed into the rough surface. She felt Luca struggling to keep his body from crushing hers as the snow thundered down around them. Out of the corner of her eye she saw the snowmobile tumbling over and over until it hurtled against another tree with a crunch of metal.

"Luca," she wanted to cry out as she felt the breath pushed from her body. "Luca, I'm sorry."

The angry torrent filled her ears, snow rushing by, banging and pummeling them, bits of ice stinging their hands and faces. They were likely going to die. And she had spent so long steeped in grief, hardened by loss, wasting all of the precious days God had given her.

"Luca," she tried again, and again her words were swallowed up by the crush.

Luca kept his arms caged around Ava, the tree bark chewing into his palms. He was not strong enough to fend off the moving mountain.

He prayed for strength, for mercy, for Ava.

The snow piled up around his legs, immobilizing him, creeping toward his chest. A few more feet and their heads would be covered, suffocating them in a blanket of brilliant white. Shoulder on fire with pain, he tried desperately to protect her.

Arms trembling he knew they had only moments

left. Snow continued to slam into his back with enough force that he found it hard to breathe.

Hang on, Ava.

He closed his eyes and concentrated on her silky hair, the softness of her small shoulder pressed against his chest. If that was the last thing he was going to feel on this earth, he could not have picked a better sensation.

As his strength failed, he gulped in one more breath of air.

The torrent suddenly stopped.

Snow continued to slide around them, but it was in lazy trickles now. The ringing in his ears subsided into quiet, broken only by the harsh sound of his own breathing. He blinked and sucked in a few more breaths.

"Ava?" he murmured in her ear.

She didn't answer and his heart quivered.

He pressed his mouth to hair. "Please answer me." He'd never wanted a reply more than he did at that moment. He'd never wanted anything in the world more than he craved the sound of her voice.

After a moment, she took a shuddering breath. "I'm okay."

He could not speak, his heart was so full of joy. "Thank you, Lord," he breathed. Wriggling back and forth, he was able to free his arms from their icy entrapment. It allowed him enough leverage to pull himself upward on a branch just above. Ava did the same and they yanked themselves free, crawling awkwardly to a higher island of snow.

Luca took Ava's hand and guided her toward the road.

They moved slowly, their feet sinking into the newly settled snow, avoiding any unnecessary movements that might set more snow in motion. When they reached the road, they could see people running toward them, Stephanie and Tate and others.

From down the mountain came the sound of sirens.

Luca held fast to Ava's hand, searching her face for a sign of what she was feeling.

Her eyes rounded in horror as she looked past him toward an irregular pile of snow.

"What is it?"

Her mouth opened but she didn't speak. Instead, she pointed to a spot on the snow he'd missed.

The spot where a hand was protruding through the icy crust.

TWENTY-THREE

Luca made it to the victim in seconds, shoveling the snow away with his hands. Tate, Stephanie and Ava joined in, freeing the body from its snowy entrapment. First the head, still covered in a ski mask, then the body, legs, arms.

Luca reached for the mask and pulled it off.

Ava cried out at the sight of Sue Agnoti, eyes closed.

Harold jogged up and dropped to his knees at her side. "Is she alive?" he croaked.

Sue answered the question for them by opening her eyes. Her gaze immediately fastened on Ava. She groaned.

Ava stared. "Sue? You shot Goren? Why would you do that?"

Sue blinked the snow from her eyes. "I was going to fix everything. Bring Bruce home."

Ava shook her head, her mouth open in shock, still staring at Sue. "You were Goren's partner?"

"Not at first. I heard Paul talking to Goren. Later

I snooped on Paul's cell phone and saw his texts to you about a treasure. I wanted to know what Paul was up to, so I contacted Goren. We made a plan to get the treasure away from Paul."

"Why?"

"Paul would waste it, squander whatever it was and besides—" she winced as she tried to move her leg "—Bruce would never accept help from Paul even if Paul had found the lost treasure of the Incas."

Luca could see in Ava's expression that she recognized that was the truth.

"So what were you going to do with the treasure, Sue?" Ava asked, voice nearly inaudible.

"I was going to save Whisper. Bring your father back home. We could all be together again, like it used to be."

Harold's mouth twisted in grief, but he held on to her hand.

Sue coughed and went on. "Goren was going to double-cross me and take the treasure for himself, so I had to stop him."

Ava's eyes filled. "All this, all these terrible choices. You made them to get my father to come back, but he doesn't love you. He's never loved you."

She shook her head. "I kept Whisper going, held things together after your mother died, all these years," Sue murmured. "He'll see my devotion once he comes home. He'll come to love me in time."

Luca looked away from the naked sorrow on Harold's face. Harold loved a woman who did not love him back. Just like Sue had wasted her life and squandered her future for a man who could not return her affection.

He felt an uncomfortable stirring in his gut as the truth bit at him.

You love Ava. You can't lie to yourself anymore.

But there was no indication that she loved him in return.

An ambulance rolled up the slope and two paramedics leaped out, carrying a rescue toboggan.

Ava and Luca moved back to allow the rescuers to do their job.

Ava walked away, back turned, gazing out on the slopes. He joined her, putting an arm around her shoulders.

"Whatever it was," Ava whispered, "whatever this treasure was is buried under a ton of snow. My uncle died because of it and Sue turned into somebody I don't recognize. I'll never even know what it was."

He squeezed her gently. "I'm sorry."

"Hey," one of the paramedics called. "Can you grab this?" They turned to find him holding the wrapped package, the one Ava had taken from the locker.

The medic held it out to them. "She had it zipped in her jacket."

Luca snatched it. Harold followed the toboggan

back to the ambulance, leaving them staring at the package.

Ava's face was white. "You open it, Luca."

He untied the string, stomach in knots as the paper slipped away.

They leaned forward to get a closer look.

Luca held up the contents.

Three books.

Romance novels.

Each bore the sticker from a long-ago garage sale.

Three for a dollar.

Ava felt like laughing. Romance novels. Three for a dollar. Another one of her uncle's crazy tricks.

She watched them load Sue up into the ambulance, next to the wounded Charlie Goren. Harold was told he could not ride along with her, so he headed for the car. He stopped before he got there and turned to Ava. "She didn't mean to hurt you or Paul. I know she loves you in her own way."

Ava's heart clenched. "Harold, I'm sorry about all this. My father never encouraged her."

He nodded. "I know. I guess sometimes the heart just goes where it wants to regardless of the facts."

And that's what had no doubt happened to Harold. The love on his face was clear, along with the hurt.

"What will you do now?" she asked gently.

He shrugged. "Stand by her, even if she doesn't

want me there." He got into the car and drove away, following the ambulance.

Her heart broke for him. She turned to find Luca talking quietly to Stephanie and Tate. She did not want to face Luca now, while her feelings felt like fragile flakes of snow. It was all over. Finally. There was no escaping that now the place would be sold. With the truth about Sue coming out, there was no friendly face here at Whisper. And Luca would go back to his treasure hunting. Back to San Francisco and another life waiting for him there.

Whatever she had felt or discovered in their mad treasure hunt would remain here, swirling in the winds of Whisper Mountain.

She heard them follow her, but she still did not turn.

"I'll go get Mack Dog. He's probably still asleep in that truck," Tate said from behind her.

That old truck. It would probably be sold for scrap. How it would grieve Uncle Paul to lose the rusty B42.

She stopped dead for one moment and then took off at a run for the garage.

"What is it?" Luca called.

She didn't answer, running as fast as she could in spite of her recent battering.

They finally caught up when she yanked open the door of the garage and barreled inside.

"What?" Luca said, taking hold of her arm.

She whirled on them. "The B42 in Mack's col-

lar. It was another one of my uncle's little jokes.
The locker number was just a diversion. It was all
about this." She gestured behind her.

Luca's eyes widened as he figured it out. "The
truck. It's a…"

"B42," Tate said. "My dad used to work with
a guy who owned one. Why didn't I think of that
earlier?"

Mack Dog woke from his nap and popped up
from the back of the vehicle. Catching sight of Tate
he leaped down and made a beeline for him. Tate
obliged him with a thorough scratching. "Have you
been guarding a treasure, boy?"

With shaking hands, Ava yanked open the door
of the truck. The interior was cold and dark. She
climbed up on the running board. She saw nothing
out of the ordinary.

Luca crawled up and slid into the driver's seat.
Ava did the same on the passenger side. She took
it all in, the worn interior, the glass with the tiny
star chip in the corner, the seat that squeaked with
every movement she made.

Her fingers found a cut in the rubber of the seat.
Tracing along the edge she discovered a slit that ran
the width of the cushion. Dropping to her knees on
the cramped floor, she carefully removed the rubber which slid easily away where it had been cut.
Heart hammering, she found a metal box that filled
the entire cushion space.

Luca's eyes shone. "Ava, you found it."

She fingered the latch that held the box closed. Nerves tingling, she opened it. Inside was a layer of thick oilcloth and underneath she saw the sturdy cover of a book, a very large volume. The cover looked to be made of leather, blackened with age. Stephanie and Tate crammed in to see.

No one spoke.

Luca pulled his sleeve over his hand and gently lifted the cover. Each massive page was divided into two columns, the first letter enlarged and elaborately decorated. Ava squinted at the text. "I can't understand it."

"That's because it's in Latin," Luca said, a slight tremble in his voice as he gingerly closed the cover. "This is a Gutenberg Bible."

Stephanie gasped. "Less than two dozen of these still exist. That makes this volume…"

"Priceless," Luca finished.

Stephanie leaned closer. "What's that? In the oilcloth?"

Ava picked up the corner of a small photo. It was a grainy picture of Ava wrapped in her mother's embrace, both of them grinning at the camera. Through a veil of tears she turned it over. On the back in Uncle Paul's dismal handwriting she could make out a single phrase.

I count myself the richest of men.

She stared at the photo as waves of love and grief crashed through her.

"He was rich, Ava, even before he found the B42,

and he finally realized it," Luca said softly. He took her hand. She was numb, her mind a hopeless jumble. The only thing she could feel was the warmth of his fingers clasping hers.

The richest of men.

Ava carefully wrapped the priceless book back up in the oilcloth, but she clung tightly to the photo. Then she stepped out of the truck and closed the door behind her.

Two days went by in a blur. The lodge was quiet now, having hosted a series of scholars and museum curators in various stages of euphoria as they photographed and packaged the precious Bible before it was taken to a bank for safekeeping. It would be donated to a museum; she was not sure which one nor did she care. She'd asked Luca to see to the arrangements.

She'd heard whispered estimates. Five million dollars. Ten. She would not sell it, this extraordinary expression of God's word, His promise that had become so real to her since that last precious time with Uncle Paul at Melody Lake.

I count myself the richest of men.

And Ava Stanton was the richest of women because she'd remembered the truth. She was not alone. God was with her and He had been all along. Through the quiet that nearly drowned her after her mother's death, the months of self-imposed isolation, He hadn't left her. And whatever her mother's choice had been, Ava knew in those last moments, God had been right by her, too, whispering words of comfort into her soul.

That same comfort now eased her pain as she signed the papers to sell Whisper, as she'd watched Luca pack up and drive away, his green eyes sparkling in her memory.

"I'll be back as soon as I get some things straightened out," he'd promised.

They both knew it was well-meaning, a gentle way for them to escape an awkward situation. She wandered around the empty kitchen, thinking of Sue and the devastating choices she'd made. But even those choices could not erase the joy and tenderness she'd felt here on Whisper Mountain.

Happy days with her mother and father.

Uncle Paul's wild adventures.

And someone else.

Another vision of Luca rippled through her memory. Ava had come to realize she loved Luca, but they were from completely different worlds. His was a life of adventure in bustling cities and her heart yearned for mountains steeped in the quiet whisper of snow.

She said a prayer for him, for his family, and picked up the small bag she'd packed.

She opened the door and gasped to find Luca standing on the other side.

"Can I come in?" he asked.

She closed her mouth. "Of course."

He wiped his feet and entered, eyes wandering around the lodge as she closed the door. Her stomach had suddenly twisted itself into knots at the sight of him.

"Thank you," she said. "For figuring out what to do with the Bible."

He laughed. "Most people I talked to were incredulous that you weren't going to sell it and become the richer than Oprah."

She smiled. "Isn't mine to sell. It's okay, though." She swallowed hard. "The agent says he's found a buyer for Whisper."

"I know."

"You do?"

He nodded, arms folded across his broad chest. "It's my father."

She started. "I guess that makes sense." She tried for a laugh. "You'll have plenty of good runs once he combines Gold Summit and Whisper."

"I guess. There's one little catch, though, a contingency to the sale."

"What's that?"

Luca moved closer and put his hands on her shoulders, his fingers sending shivers up her spine.

"He bought it because I asked him to."

"You knew it would be a good investment?"

"The best."

She felt a shiver run up her back. "What's the contingency?"

"It's going to be a wedding present."

"For whom?"

"I'm hoping…" He was close now, so close she could smell the musky scent of his aftershave. "For us."

Her mouth fell open. "What?"

He moved his hands to gently cup her face. "I love you, Ava. I've loved you since we were sixteen years old and I watched you fly down that mountain. Our lives got in the way for a while, but now it's time to fix that."

She clutched at his hands, her pulse buzzing in her veins. "Luca, we're so different, I…"

"You're right," he said, pressing a kiss to her temple and then one on each cheek. "You're quiet and thoughtful and at home in the middle of nowhere. And I'm loud and impulsive and I like to be where the chaos is, and you know what?" He kissed her again, this time on the tip of her nose. "I like it like that."

"But your business, Treasure Seekers."

"Whisper will be my remote office. I can find treasures just as well from here as San Francisco. I think Victor and Stephanie will enjoy not having me around all the time. They tell me I get on their nerves now and then."

She dared to allow herself to entertain the possibility that he loved her. Luca Gage, the boy she'd beaten down the mountain so many times, loved her. Tears prickled her eyes. "What do I say?" she murmured.

He pressed his mouth to her ear. "Say you love me and you'll marry me. Together we'll make Whisper into the gem of the Sierras again."

A jumble of emotions cascaded through her body. "I…"

He traced her ear with his mouth. "Ava Stanton, I love you. I love you. I love you."

Light flooded her soul like the clouds parting after a winter storm. Brilliant, clear, jubilant.

"I love you, Luca," she whispered, letting the joy cascade through her body, filling every dark place with light. "And I will marry you."

His voice was hoarse as he embraced her. "In the words of your uncle, I consider myself the richest of men."

Ava lifted her face to his, knowing that she, too, had finally found her treasure.

* * * * *

Dear Reader,

April is my favorite month because every year I give myself a glorious birthday present—I plant my garden. Oh, how I love tucking in those vegetable plants (always too many tomato bushes) and herbs (I've learned to protect the basil with broken eggshells to discourage the snails) and a row of giant sunflowers. The sunflowers are to beckon the bees and I don't even mind the little finches that come down to eat the leaves. It's funny how over the years I'm coming to realize that instead of those nifty presents of jewelry, clothes, etc., the greatest treasures are the things of God, temporary though they may be, that wash my life with joy.

I have enjoyed writing this Treasure Seekers series about folks who pursue those worldly treasures—pearls, violins, paintings—and in the process discover that relationships are by far the greatest blessing. My father has always said blessings aren't free. He's right about that. Blessings sometimes come with heartache and certainly require a lot of hard work (my garden is a case in point!), but those blessings give us a tiny taste of the abundant treasures God has in store for us someday.

Thank you very much for blessing me by reading this book. Your kind notes and emails are surely treasures to me. You can reach me via my webpage at www.danamentink.com and there is a physical address there also for those who prefer corresponding by mail.

Dana Mentink

Questions for Discussion

1. Melody Lake is a place steeped in memories for Ava. Is there a place in your life that evokes such strong feelings? Share about it.

2. Uncle Paul is a man of dubious character, yet he is a source of comfort and support to Ava. How is it possible for a person to be both?

3. Ava's family has owned Whisper Mountain Resort for decades. Would you have made the same decision to sell that Ava did?

4. Why do you think Luca always experiences a letdown after he reaches his goal of finding treasure? Have you ever experienced something similar after you attained a goal you set for yourself?

5. Uncle Paul is devoted to Mack Dog. Tell about an animal that you are/were close to.

6. Ava is crushed by her mother's apparent suicide. What Bible verse or verses could provide comfort to a person who had experienced such a loss?

7. In view of Uncle Paul's treatment of others, why does Bully help him?

8. Luca says, "Strong women are a pain." What attracts him to Ava in spite of his statement?

9. Ava is awed by a landscape so beautiful it could only have been made by God Himself. Have you ever had similar feelings? Describe what you saw and felt.

10. Paul was after a fabulous pearl. What are some other worldly treasures people pursue? In our culture, what treasures are valued the most?

11. Goren has been taken advantage of by Paul. Have you ever been in a similar situation with a friend? How did you overcome your feelings?

12. Ava realizes that her good memories will be forever entwined with her loss. How can we find solace in our God-given treasures even when they are no longer physically with us?

13. Uncle Paul counted himself rich, although he died without profiting from his treasure. How would he have lived his life differently if he came to this realization earlier?

14. What treasure do you think Luca, Stephanie, Tate and Ava will hunt for next?

15. What are the greatest treasures in your own life?

LARGER-PRINT BOOKS!

GET 2 FREE LARGER-PRINT NOVELS PLUS 2 FREE MYSTERY GIFTS

RIVETING INSPIRATIONAL ROMANCE

Larger-print novels are now available...

YES! Please send me 2 FREE LARGER-PRINT Love Inspired® Suspense novels and my 2 FREE mystery gifts (gifts are worth about $10). After receiving them, if I don't wish to receive any more books, I can return the shipping statement marked "cancel." If I don't cancel, I will receive 4 brand-new novels every month and be billed just $4.99 per book in the U.S. or $5.49 per book in Canada. That's a savings of at least 23% off the cover price. It's quite a bargain! Shipping and handling is just 50¢ per book in the U.S. and 75¢ per book in Canada.* I understand that accepting the 2 free books and gifts places me under no obligation to buy anything. I can always return a shipment and cancel at any time. Even if I never buy another book, the two free books and gifts are mine to keep forever.

110/310 IDN FVZ7

Name	(PLEASE PRINT)

Address	Apt. #

City	State/Prov.	Zip/Postal Code

Signature (if under 18, a parent or guardian must sign)

Mail to the **Harlequin® Reader Service:**
IN U.S.A.: P.O. Box 1867, Buffalo, NY 14240-1867
IN CANADA: P.O. Box 609, Fort Erie, Ontario L2A 5X3

Are you a current subscriber to Love Inspired Suspense books and want to receive the larger-print edition?
Call 1-800-873-8635 or visit www.ReaderService.com.

* Terms and prices subject to change without notice. Prices do not include applicable taxes. Sales tax applicable in N.Y. Canadian residents will be charged applicable taxes. Offer not valid in Quebec. This offer is limited to one order per household. Not valid for current subscribers to Love Inspired Suspense larger-print books. All orders subject to credit approval. Credit or debit balances in a customer's account(s) may be offset by any other outstanding balance owed by or to the customer. Please allow 4 to 6 weeks for delivery. Offer available while quantities last.

Your Privacy—The Harlequin® Reader Service is committed to protecting your privacy. Our Privacy Policy is available online at www.ReaderService.com or upon request from the Harlequin Reader Service.

We make a portion of our mailing list available to reputable third parties that offer products we believe may interest you. If you prefer that we not exchange your name with third parties, or if you wish to clarify or modify your communication preferences, please visit us at www.ReaderService.com/consumerschoice or write to us at Harlequin Reader Service Preference Service, P.O. Box 9062, Buffalo, NY 14269. Include your complete name and address.

ReaderService.com

Manage your account online!

- Review your order history
- Manage your payments
- Update your address

*We've designed
the Harlequin® Reader Service
website just for you.*

Enjoy all the features!

- Reader excerpts from any series
- Respond to mailings and special monthly offers
- Discover new series available to you
- Browse the Bonus Bucks catalog
- Share your feedback

Visit us at:

ReaderService.com